THE
FORGOTTEN
Their Champion Companion Novel

K.A. KNIGHT

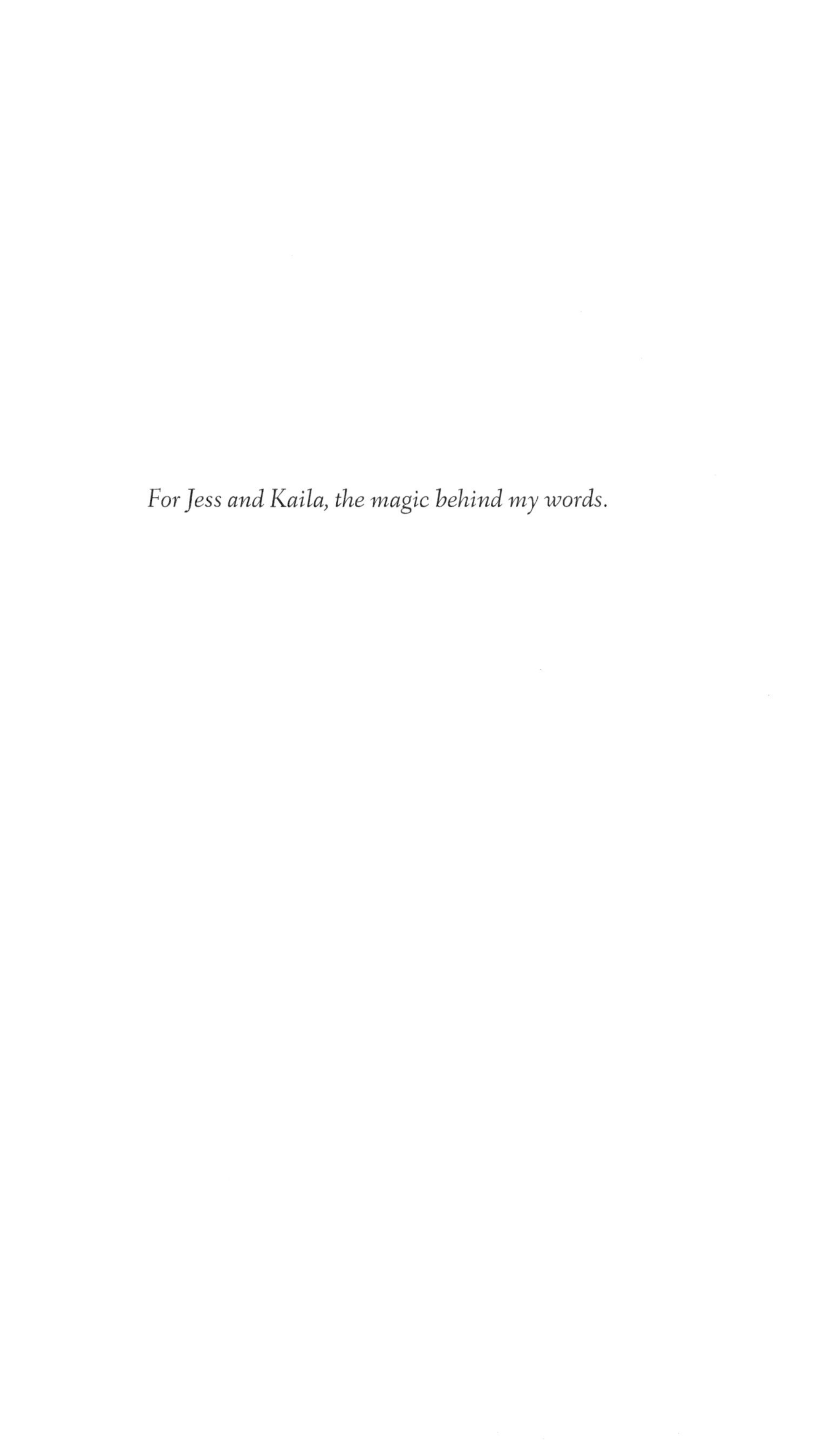

For Jess and Kaila, the magic behind my words.

WORSHIPPERS
OF THE SUN

THE FORGOTTEN

THE
LOST

PARADI

TOWN OF
SPRING

D E A D   S E A

THE
WASTELAND
THEIR CHAMPION SERIES

ERSERKERS
THE RING
THE SEEKERS
REEVES
THE RIM
HE CITIES
DEAD SEA

Author Note

Please be aware that this book contains scenes that some may find triggering.

If you have any concerns, please skip to the last page of the book, where I've given a more specific warning that does contain some spoilers.

Rules of Paradise

All must work
All must contribute

If you leave,
you may never come back

Paradise is the new world,

To question that is to
question the law.

Chapter 1
Just Friends

With a mischievous grin, I spin away from the incoming guards and into the med bay. I should be in class, but I hate water systems. Learning it is so boring. So, I snuck out to meet Evan. Looking around his usual place of hiding, my grin stretches when I spot him bent over reading some boring medical book. For as long as we have been friends, he has been trying to convince me to join him in medicine, but it has never appealed to me, being locked away down here and depended on so much. I dream of bigger things, things he tells me to keep quiet. The type of things that make him roll his eyes and get that look on his face that reminds me of the age gap between us. Three years isn't a lot, but down here it probably feels like a lifetime.

He is so structured and ruled, liking his own peace and quiet and the boringness of every day. Whereas I am the total opposite, he tells me I have my head in the clouds dreaming of a world that doesn't exist, but how can he not want to know what's outside? To see for himself, explore. The world might have died, but I am betting the human race survived, it's just who we are. I asked him once why he hung around me if he thought my dreams were stupid, he told me my hope was the light in the grey. I never asked again.

Rolling my eyes when he doesn't even turn around to see who it is, I decide to sneak up on him. That's the one thing I have going for me, I am quiet when I need to be, a trait hard earned from sneaking around down here. When I am close enough to smell his mint body wash, I lean down close to his ear. "Boo!"

He jumps, fumbling with his book and letting out a girly scream that sends me into hysterics. Falling back to lean on the medical bed I watch him through tear filled eyes. He turns to me, his short messy brown hair moving with him as his emerald green eyes lock on mine with anger. "Damn it Pip, you scared the shit out of me!"

Groaning at the nickname, I hop up on the bed and stare at him with my innocent smile. It makes him grunt as he bends down to pick up the book, which has to be thicker than both of his arms put together and that is saying something because Evan is shredded. I don't know why, it's not like he has to fight or go on patrol, but he likes to keep fit.

His wide muscly arms are covered in half-finished tribal sleeves, the ink extending up his arms, across his chest, and around his neck. His eyebrow piercing glints in the light and I freeze when I spot the new addition to his lip. He has his usual black army boots on, tucked into black cargo pants, his white t-shirt sticks to his chest and I have to wipe my mouth to check for drool. Not that he would notice, I don't think he even knows I am a girl.

Evan and I grew up in the same section of Paradise, the orphanage, which was basically a forgotten room cleared for him and me. My parents were patrollers who were killed out there, something that was explained to me in excruciating detail to try and squish the longing to see the outside world growing in my chest. Evan's mum and dad left Paradise so long ago I can barely remember them, they told him they would carve out a better life for him out there. That it was wrong living down here, just surviving, they wanted to live.

So, they left, faced the Wastes even though they knew they might never come back. All he has left of them is the rose tattoos covering the back of each hand, a promise that they will come back for him. They never did. I guess our screwed up past made us fast friends. I was new to the orphanage section, which was basically a massive room with beds shoved so close together you can almost touch. Only one bathroom is attached. A place to leave the kids that don't matter, but Evan sure proved them wrong. I knew he would. Ever since he was young, he wanted to be a doctor, to help people. I never understood why, it's not like he's a people person, but all he would say is that he did it for the people he loved, whatever that meant. Anyway, we have been inseparable ever since. However, as we grew up my feelings for him turned deeper, and I started noticing things a best friend shouldn't. But to him, I will always be Pip, the little girl he used to sing and cuddle to sleep when she cried for her dead parents. Shaking my head and the depressing thoughts away I point at his lip.

"New?"

He dusts off the book before setting it gently down on the workstation behind him and swivelling to face me. "Yeah, I was bored last night and decided to see if I could."

I giggle at that, I asked him to pierce my ears once and I have never seen such outrage in somebody's eyes before he snatched away his gun and walked away like Misty was chasing him.

Swinging my legs back and forth on the bed I look at the floor. My long brown hair falls into my face and with a puff, I blow it away. Freezing, I hold my breath as a tattooed hand appears in front of my face. With the utmost care, Evan brushes away my hair and puts it behind my ear, smiling at me softly. I return it as his hand lingers against my cheek. Gulping, I beg myself not to lean into his touch. His green eyes change and my heart stutters as I see desire burning in them, but as quick as it came, it disappears, and he drops his hand and turns away like I am diseased. He has been doing that a lot lately.

Gritting my teeth, I twist my mum's wedding ring on my finger nervously. "So, what we doing today, Doc? Dissecting cannibals, stitching patrols who shot themselves in the foot?"

Without looking at me he turns on his computer and wiggles the mouse. "Nope, you are going to class."

Groaning, I fall back dramatically on the bed and stare at the boring white ceiling, just like every other ceiling down here. "C'mon Evvie, don't be so boring. I only have three months left and we both know I am not going into the water systems engineering." I shiver at the last, seriously? Who would pick cleaning out shit as their job for the rest of their lives?

"Exactly Piper, so stop being such a brat and just go to your classes and stop bugging me at work," he snaps, and I sit bolt upright glaring at his hunched form. Brat? Bugging? Ugh, Mr. Mardy is obviously in one of his lovely moods today.

Hopping down from the bed I throw a glare at him, which can I just say is lost on him...it was a good glare too. All narrowed eyed with deep intensity, boy would have shitted a brick but sadly he remains staring intently at his scans ignoring my strop. "Sorry for bothering you with my bratty ways, your dickness," I say before turning to leave.

"Dickness, really?" he calls, and I glance over my shoulder to see he hasn't even looked away from the screen, even if I can hear the smile in his voice. What a cum bucket.

"Yep, it's like your highness cause you are super stuck up, but also a dick. So dickness, maybe you should get that tattooed on you next," I fume, spinning around again.

"Where are you going, Pip?" he asks and I don't stop this time, unwilling to let him see the hurt in my expression. He has been pushing me away more and more, and it doesn't get any easier.

"To hang out with someone who actually appreciates me and doesn't treat me like I am shit on the bottom of his shoe." Stomping out the door I hear him swear as he tries to come after me, it makes me smile a little. We can never stay mad at each other for long, and sometimes it takes me spelling it out for him to realise what he has done.

"Come on, Pip. I didn't mean—oh hello, General Kertol." I spin and see the Paradise guard's general standing with his arms behind his back and an expectant expression on his face, which is swinging between me and Evan before he ignores me completely and turns to face Evan.

"Doctor Sencal, we need your assistance."

"Of course, General. I will be right there," Evan says smoothly.

With a nod the general walks away, not even uttering a hello to me. I flip him the bird with both hands, immature, but it makes me feel better. I look at Evan to see him glaring at me even as his lips twitch.

"We can carry on this argument later, Pip."

Huffing, I turn around. "Sure, whatever you say, your royal dickness."

Happy I got the last word, I flounce away in search of some- thing fun to do, screw Evan and his attitude. I can't keep letting him get to me, and one of these days he will push too hard or say some- thing he can't take back.

I groan as Todd fumbles against my chest, his clumsy hands looking for my breasts as he kisses me without breathing. Okay, so he's not the best kisser, or the smartest semen in the stream, but he sure is good looking and he does take my mind off Evan for a little bit. Plus, he sure can wear that guard uniform. Turning my head to the side, I roll my eyes as he pants into my neck and moans like a porn star. Really dude, I haven't even touched his junk and he sounds like he is going to explode like a shaken can of coke.

Looking around him while he fondles my breast and dry humps me like a dog on speed, I soon get bored. The room we are in is— you guessed it—all white! Gasp! It was probably a water storage plant at one point, but they never use it anymore and all the teenagers sneak down here to hang out. I am regretting that deci- sion as Todd, the numbnuts of Paradise, dribbles down my neck. Okay, time to go.

"Todd, I have a meeting with my selection advisor," I say and push him away. He groans and moves back, looking disappointed.

"Fine, you want to meet later?" he asks hopefully, cupping his crotch as if I couldn't understand the implication.

"We'll see." Reaching down I grab my jacket and leave before he can corner me.

Sauntering to the classroom where I am supposed to meet the uptight adviser, I just turn a corner when I freeze in shock. My heart stops and I feel like I might faint. They don't notice me, too busy feeling each other up in the corridor, but I can see from the tattooed hands and arms who it is. Evan and some skank. He leans his head back against the wall and stops her with one hand, but I have seen enough. Spinning so they don't see me, I flee as the tears start to fall. It's stupid and only makes me angrier at myself. I mean I was just doing the same thing, but Evan doesn't fuck around. Never has, hell I've never even seen him with a woman. Something about him always being too busy. He must care about her. The thought stops me, and I lean against the wall before sliding down to sit on my arse. All my hopes and stupid dreams of him finally noticing me and giving us a go evaporate. God, I am so stupid. Of course, he would never notice me.

I sit there for a while, throwing myself a pity party before I wipe my eyes and drag myself to my feet. Fuck him, I have survived a lot in this bloody life, I can survive losing him too.

The thought drives me, but it also makes me realise I have been waiting. Just lingering like I knew something was coming, tugging on his doctor's coat the whole time like a child with a comfort blanket. Never making a real decision for myself. Well fuck that, it's time I decided how I imagine my future. I just hope I can be grown up enough to keep him in it, just as a friend.

Chapter 2

Beast Man

I manage to avoid Evan for two days. It feels strange, usually we spend every waking minute together, but I need to get my own emotions in check before I do. I know I have projected my feelings onto him, and it's not fair he pays the price. He never gave me any indication he thought of me romantically, and I know right now he will be upset wondering what he did, but I need to be selfish for a moment before I can let him in again and even then, we need to make some boundaries so this never happens again. I spend those two days staying busy, and I meet with my adviser and go through all my options. It wasn't until he was outlining what a patrol career would entail that I knew what I wanted. It gives me everything, the chance to see outside and still come back safe, while experiencing adventure and life outside of the bunker. It also allows me some time away from Evan, where I can just be me. I know it's the right path for me, it sends my heart into overdrive and for the first time in a long time, I am excited about something.

My advisor scoffed and told me women don't become guards or do patrols, but I will prove him wrong. I have been coasting through classes, just learning enough to pass, but I know once I set my mind to something, nothing will stand in my way, because what I don't have in talent, I make up for in stubbornness.

I leave the advisor meeting with a new hop in my step and steel running down my spine. I have a month to prove I will make a good patrol, or I get placed into whatever role they think will best serve the community. I can't let that happen. I know I would wither and die, dramatic but true. I am a dreamer, a believer, and doing the same boring meaningless job every day will kill something inside of me.

That's why I go straight to the guard's section of the bunker and wait for Todd to finish his training class. Leaning against the wall, I spend my time checking out the guard's asses as they walk past.

"Piper?" comes a hesitant voice. Looking up from the peachy rear I am checking out, I smile at Todd. He is standing in the open doorway to the gym with a towel raised to his sweaty face.

"Hey." Wow, lame. He raises his eyebrow and steps away from the door, raising the towel and wiping his face before putting it back around his neck.

"You okay?" he asks worriedly. It makes me feel horrible, maybe I have been too harsh on him. He has always been nice to me, and so what if he isn't the brightest, he works hard and actually has the time of day for people. I can see the worry dancing in his eyes and it only serves to make me feel worse.

"Yeah, I'm fine." Blowing out a breath I hold out my hand. "Can we start again? Hi, I'm Piper. I can be a stone-cold bitch, I love coffee and watching the night sky."

He hesitates, but a slow grin forms on his handsome face. "Hi Piper, nice to meet you. I'm Todd, I like music and women who know what they want."

We share a grin and he step closer to me, and I feel my heart- beat speed up. "Can we go somewhere to talk?" I ask and he nods, looking around and spotting the other guards lingering and watching us.

"Come on, I know the perfect place." I smile and we walk side by side. It's nice, and it feels good, like I am letting someone else in. We might never be best friends, but I know he will help me if I need it.

"So, you want me to train you in self-defence and what to expect outside?" Todd asks for the fourth time, and I have to hold myself back from hitting my own head against the wall. Dude might be nice, but he can be stupid.

"Yes...please," I grit out and remind myself of my promise to be nicer.

Todd sighs and slumps on the chair opposite me. He dragged me to his room and jumped in the shower. I am betting he didn't expect me to talk to him from my perched position on the counter. Dude acted like a girl, covering up and stuff. He seems more comfortable now though...too comfortable.

"Eh, Todd?" I say and he looks up from running the towel through his hair.

"Yeah?"

"Your legs are open, and you have nothing on but a towel," I point out helpfully. He glances down and his eyes shoot wide when he sees that it has slipped, and I can see his pet iguana.

"Fuck!" He quickly covers up as his face turns bright red. "Dude, it's cool. It was a nice enough penis, like congratulations

I guess?"

He blinks at me owlishly. "Not helping Piper."

I hold my hands up and sit back. "Sorry, sorry. Just thought pointing out that your balls are very nice and symmetrical might ease your embarrassment."

"Okay, moving on," he grunts out, his face turning even redder.

This is a fun game, but I decide to take pity on him. "Can you do it?" I ask.

It takes him the longest time to think about it and when he finally does, he shakes his head, sending disappointment coursing through me. Damn, back to square one.

"But I might know someone who can..." Eagerly I lean forward, and he grimaces.

"He's a scary motherfucker though, and will probably say no."

"Let me handle that, who can say no to this cute face?" I stick

out my tongue and blink innocently, and he looks like he is holding in a fart.

"Sure thing, let me just grab some clothes and I will take you to him."

Fuck me sideways and hose me down, he is a beast. We aren't talking the hairy kind, but the kind that makes your panties wet and your nipples hard. Dark brown hair, reaching below his ears and mussed, merges into a trimmed dark brown beard. His face is square and beautiful in a deadly way. He's tall, way too fucking tall, and built like a brick shit house. He's older than me, probably older than even Evan, and his arms are thicker than my entire torso. Anger seems to follow him, giving everyone a clear fuck off vibe.

I am pretty sure I'm drooling from my mouth and my sausage wallet, but damn!

"Earth to Piper." Todd waves his hand in front of my eyes with a funny look on his face.

"Uh huh, man tits," I blurt, before snapping my mouth shut and looking at Todd. He snorts before bursting into laughter. I can't help but join in and that's how Mr. Wet Dreams finds me, leaning on Todd with tears streaming down my face as I snort like a pig. Hot.

He lifts the bottom of his shirt and wipes his sweaty face, giving me a good view of the eight pack and adonis belt carved into his skin. This man is pure lethal power, and it shows. But he also seems too rough, too...other to be a paradise guard. Everyone down here is so clean cut and good, but this man looks like he would show up covered in blood and not apologise. Grunting, he grips the shirt and rips it off. Scars, both faded and newer looking, criss-cross randomly on his chest like he has been in a lot of near-death situations. When he turns to throw the shirt on the floor, I notice his back is covered in long, thick brutal looking scars, but it only adds to the man before me. He's savage, I knew that coming in, but seeing his survival and fight carved onto his body has me shifting uncomfortably, trying to ease the ache between my thighs. He is all power, dark and danger- ous, and I want it all. I want that fury aimed at me.

"What the fuck do you want?" he asks, striding towards us and towering over me, looking down at both me and Todd with a blank expression. He makes Todd look like a child and as his muscles clench, I bet he could snap me in two without breaking a sweat. The word fuck coming from his mouth only makes me sweat harder, holy shit.

"Err- hi, Jago, Piper here wanted to meet you." With that, Todd pushes me forward, sacrificing me to the angry giant and turns and walks quickly away. Pussy.

He looks down at me, his eyes so intense I gasp. They look like they are on fire. A deep brown closest to the pupil fades to an amber on the outside, and they are centered on me, staring into me. Have you ever looked into someone's eyes and just know they can see all your secrets? Well, this look sends shivers right down my spine. "What do you want?" he repeats, not in a rude way, but more like he is already thinking of other things he should be doing.

"I want you to train me," I say bluntly, already recognizing him as someone who doesn't do small talk and bullshit. It's refreshing.

"No." With that, he turns and walks back to the mats.

"Not even going to think about it?" I call, starting to get pissy. "No," he reiterates, as he starts boxing the bag and dancing around it. For someone so big, he sure is light on his feet. His brush off only adds to the anger burning in the pit of my stomach, one that started when I saw Evan kissing that woman.

"Just because you are hot doesn't mean you can be a cummuffin!" I shout before making my way back into his line of sight. "Train me, I want to go on patrol and we both know they won't accept a woman, not unless someone vouches for me. I have a month." He continues moving around and I move with him. "I will do everything you say, I will work harder than any other recruit. Please, just give me a chance." He stops and pants, still staring at the bag. I watch his jaw move before he turns and stalks along the mat.

"No, the outside isn't any place for a little girl. Go work in hairdressing or beauty," he dismisses me, and my eyes narrow. That motherfucking cuntholio. I don't know what comes over me, apart from that I want to prove him wrong. I am betting he never expected a 'little girl' to attack him from behind, but when you are an orphan girl, you do learn some moves. Plus, I dated an armoury recruit, let's just say the roughhousing turned me on.

Light on my feet I run at him, at the last second, I slide and kick his feet out from under him. It's not smooth or refined like I am betting his fighting is, but it does the trick. He goes tumbling down, but I don't even manage to move from my back on the mat before he flips and has me pinned with my hands above my head, his face inches from mine. Fuck he's fast, I twist experimentally, and he doesn't even budge. It should scare me, but my heart is racing and my chest is heaving for another reason.

"How do you get out of this position?" he demands, his fiery eyes pinning me to the spot just like his body. It takes an embarrass- ingly long time for his words to penetrate my mind but when they do, I think it through. He bangs my hands back down on the mat and growls, "Concentrate."

Grunting, I slowly bring my legs up. I quickly wrap them around his neck and yank backwards. The move is unexpected because he falls back, which drags me up until I have him pinned. I see respect bloom in his eyes before he squashes it.

"Good, but this hold is easy to break out of," he says, before bringing his arms up through the triangle my legs are making around his neck and pushing. My thighs shake with the effort, but I gasp and fall away, he is too strong.

He sits up slowly and we watch each other. "You're weak, but you're small and fast, there are moves you would be able to pull, it's not all about brute strength."

With that he stands, and grabs his shirt from the side and starts to walk away, leaving me confused on the mat. "Does that mean you will train me?" I shout and I hear him laugh, the deep rough sound sending shivers through my body.

"No," he yells back, and then he is gone, and I fall back onto the mat with a groan, but I can't help but smile. He doesn't know what he just got himself into, I am not giving up. Stalker mode initiated.

The next morning, I am in the gym bright and early in my workout clothes. Some stretchy black skin-tight trousers and a black tank top. I bribed Todd to tell me Jago's schedule. It turns out he is one of the lead patrols, but he only ever goes out alone. He's a legend among the guards, he doesn't work well with others, and the Paradise guards stay well away. He wasn't even born down here, he came from outside. No one knows from where, he just showed up one day on patrols half dead and they took him in. That is a miracle in itself. Rumours and stories circle him, and I find myself wanting to know the truth. He is also very regimented, the dude obviously has a thing for schedules. He trains every day from six to eight, then breakfast after that before he trains other recruits. Then he works late evening to night patrol. He is like a machine, I wonder if he ever sleeps. He probably just reboots like a computer or some weird shit.

So yeah, here I am like a stalker waiting outside the gym for him. I smiled sweetly at the cafeteria guy, he's had a crush on me forever which I thoroughly exploit for that synthetic coffee shit. So, I have two in my hands waiting for beefcake to turn up, and like clockwork he does.

When he sees me, he grunts, but I see the corner of his lip quirk up before he masks it. He goes as if to walk past me and I slide in front of the door, thrusting the coffee at him. He eyes it like it's an alien. "You shouldn't drink that shit."

I gasp dramatically and pull it to my chest, shielding it. I whisper down to it, "Don't listen to Meany McMean pants, he didn't mean it. You are the elixir of life and I will never give you up."

He eyes me strangely before trying to walk past me once more. He sighs when I block his way again. "You aren't going to give up, are you?"

"Nope, I am delightful like that. One of my teachers referred to me as stubborn as a tick on a tit," I supply helpfully, and down one coffee even as it burns my mouth before bringing the other to my mouth. I blame the coffee, since I have my hands full and I can't stop him when he grips my hips and picks me up, before depositing me next to the door. Then without speaking, he enters the gym and leaves me there gaping at him.

"More words than most people have got sweetie, but why don't you try a man who might be interested." I turn and stare at the guard who is entering the gym. He winks and slips inside. Ugh, what a prick, like women only go after a man for one reason? Can't a girl just want them to teach them how to become a badass? Honestly, it's a little insulting.

Downing the rest of the coffee, I dispose of the reusable cups in the container in the corner before entering the gym. Damn, you can almost taste the testosterone in here. It's basically a giant circle jerk.

Looking around, I only have one thought—penises, penises everywhere. Wrinkling my nose at the smell of sweat, I look around for my target. I notice a few men staring at me, but I ignore them and hone in on Jago. He is in the back corner and it looks like his reputation precedes him. Every other inch of the gym is crawling with training guards, but there is a whole circle of empty space around him, and the men nearest eye him warily. Me? I trot up to him, ignoring the incredulous looks being thrown my way and the guys checking me out. I nearly reach him but a buff looking dumbbell dude steps in in front of me, smiling at me in a way that is obviously supposed to be seductive.

"Hey sweetness, did you want to play? I'd be happy to oblige." He lowers his voice as I look him up and down, he puffs out his chest and I have to hold in laugh. But why do guys always call you something along the lines of sweet? The only thing sweet about me is the fake sugar running through my veins from the coffee...

"No thanks, looks like you play with yourself enough," I quip, before stepping around him and jumping up on the chair next to Jago. He is lifting weights, a mirror at his side, and I sit swinging my legs back and forth watching him. Eventually he must get sick of me because he puts the weight down and eyes me right back. "You look ridiculous," he comments before turning back around.

"If by ridiculous you mean ridiculously hot, then yes, I do," I supply and go back to watching him. He moves like a well-oiled machine, pure strength as he pushes his body. He doesn't come here to show off like the others, he comes here to challenge himself, that much is obvious.

"What?" he grunts as he lifts the weight.

I tilt my head and stare at him. "I just realised you don't care about showing off. For you, this is to push yourself, to make yourself the best you can be."

He freezes, before dropping the weight and looking at me strangely. "What makes you say that?"

"Well for starters, you don't go around showing off how much you can bench. You don't care if the others are looking—hell, there could be a group surrounding you and you would feel more uncom- fortable than by yourself. I see that fire in your eyes, you want to go harder, be better," I finish, before whistling as I look around the gym. The silence stretches and I look back to see him looking shocked. "What?" I ask confused.

He stares at me for so long I start to fidget, twisting my mum's ring on my finger. Finally, he grunts and stands up. "You best go home now, things are about to get dirty."

I grin and jump up. "Yes, the best type of fun! Will there be jelly? Mud wrestling? Whose arse are we kicking? Will there be blood? I can't wait!" I bounce up and down, the coffee kicking in. He looks down at me, arching one eyebrow before reaching out and putting a hand on my head, stilling my movements. "Don't say I didn't warn you."

I nod and follow him as he marches to the mat, where the other fighters are slowly clearing away. When he stops, I run into his back and grunt, before falling back on my ass. Jumping up I hold my hands up when every eye turns my way. "I'm okay, dude's back is like a wall is all."

He groans before turning around, throwing me over his shoulder and striding away from the mats. When he deems it a safe distance, he plops me onto a chair and points in my face. "Stay." I nod.

He turns and walks away, but glances back like he doesn't trust me not to move. When he sees me, I wave and I watch his lips quirk again before he turns back around, then his face is wiped clean like I imagined it.

"Who's first?" he grumbles, standing in the middle of the mat as at least thirty guards look between each other. I can almost taste the anticipation in the air.

I jump when a hand lands on my shoulder, and looking up, I smile at Todd. "What's going on?" I ask curiously, glancing back to the mats to see three men join Jago.

"Every day the guards test their strength against him, it's a running game. No one has managed to take him down yet," he explains, crossing his arms and watching with everyone else.

"No one?" I question in shock, thinking back to yesterday when I got lucky.

"Nope, the guy's patrol name is Beast, because he fights fast and dirty. He doesn't give a shit about holding back or rules. Doesn't make you friends, but he doesn't care."

I nod as Todd speaks, and in breathless admiration, I watch as within two minutes he dispatches the first three guards without even breaking a sweat. He crunched one's nose, knocked one out, and I am pretty sure the third has broken ribs. Todd is right, he fights dirty. Once you are in his sights he attacks, no waiting, and no hesi- tation. He goes in for the kill every time.

He waits for the next lot, and this time four step onto the mat. Big, mean looking bastards. He just blinks at them and waits. One moves to attack, and Jago is gone, like lightning he darts around and wraps his arm around the other guy's neck, choking him out. One of the others goes in, circling behind him and trying for a cheap shot. Jago simply throws the man in his arms clear across the room and turns around with a ninja kick to the side, catching the man in the face. He goes down hard and doesn't stir. The two others yell and go at him. They exchange blows, him blocking them both and scoring hits on them, until they are panting. One's arms falter and he upper- cuts him and turns his attention to the remaining man. They circle each other and Jago grins, before reaching down and jerking the mat, sending the man tumbling. He is on him in a second, pounding his head into the mat, again and again, until he lets go and the man doesn't move.

Standing he looks around, this time a trickle of sweat drips down his chest. When no one else steps forward, I see his shoulders relax. A stupid idea hits me, seriously stupid. Like, don't do it, but if it pays off, I can use it to make him train me and if it doesn't, I am no worse off, apart from having my ass handed to me but... shit I know it's stupid.

Does that stop me from doing it? Hell no.

Leaping from the chair, I stride with confidence that I don't feel onto the mat. He hears me coming, his head tilting. When he turns, I see the flash in his eyes before he narrows them on me.

"No," he growls out.

I roll my shoulders and bounce on my feet. "You submitting to me?" I grin and whispers start amongst the other guards. He turns his glare on them before looking back at me.

"I am not beating up a girl," he intonates slowly, like I am stupid.

"Good, then I will beat you up." With that I fling myself at him, going for the element of surprise again. It's all I have on him. He outweighs me, is faster, stronger, and a hell of a better fighter.

He dodges at the last minute and I spin and jump again. He holds his arm out mid jump, knocking into my chest and sending me flying as the breath is knocked out of me.

I get back up slower this time and he rolls his eyes. "Stay down," he says and I shake my head.

"Make me," I dare him, and I see that flash again, before he unleashes himself. I can still tell he's holding himself back, but he doesn't wait for me to attack. He tries to put me down, hard and fast. He darts in and elbows my stomach, sending me reeling, and then he kicks out at my legs, dropping me to my arse. I grumble but get up slowly, ignoring the pain in my stomach. His eyebrow rises when I get to my feet, but he comes at me again. I manage to slip around some of the punches and I dart in and punch his stomach, which seems to hurt me more than him, but I see the surprise in his eyes, and he regards me more carefully as we stare at each other. One minute he is still, the next he is whirling towards me. I duck and weave the best I can, stum- bling back to avoid his punches. I see him balance on one leg and jump as he kicks out, only to miss the punch aimed at my head. It connects with my chin and sends me sprawling, and I am pretty sure I see stars. Face down into the mat I push up and rest my forehead on it. "Stay down," he orders, and when I slowly turn my head, I spot him crouched next to me.

I ignore him and push to my feet, wobbling this time. My body hurts and my muscles are shaking. He sighs, but I see him grin before he stands again. This time he holds his hands out to the side and waits.

I dart in once or twice, testing him and when he doesn't react, I feign left before punching out at his neck. His eyes widen and he gasps when I connect, his hands coming up to protect his face as he struggles to breathe. I take his hesitation and knee his junk, not a nice move, but he does fight dirty and so will I. He falls to his knees with a wheeze, his hands going to his cock, covering it protectively.

I grin but when I see the look on his face, it fades into a squeal. "Run," he growls.

Shit, shit, shit, fucking shit on a dick and spin.

He flies at me, wrapping his arms around me from behind as I try to get away. He lifts me before flinging me across the mat. I roll and groan as I stop. Fuck, that is going to hurt tomorrow.

I get to my feet again as I see him coming towards me, his muscles bunching. My head is ringing at this point and my eyes blur- ring, it makes me sluggish and I don't react quickly enough as an elbow comes towards my face, at the last minute he stops it and I stand there panting with his elbow two inches from my nose.

"I don't beat up girls," he mutters quietly, stepping away. I wobble a step after him, and he sighs.

"Stop."

I ignore him and he shakes his head before his elbow makes contact with the side of my head. I go down hard, I can feel uncon- sciousness flirting at the edge of my vision, but I try to fight it. If I pass out, he will never train me. I don't know how I know, but I do.

So, I struggle and fight as I lay there, and eventually it fades and the pain returns, making me gasp.

I look up to see him sitting next to me. "You okay?" he asks softly.

"Never better," I cough out, my eyes wincing as it pulls on my bruised ribs. He rolls his eyes and stands, holding his hand out to me. I know this moment is important, so I reach up and he pulls me to my feet softly, steadying me when I stumble. When he is sure I won't fall, he walks back to his corner, leaving me in the middle of the mat. I see the other guards staring at me in shock before, with a yell from Jago, they quickly get back to what they were doing.

Something drops down my chin and I reach up and wince when I feel my swollen lip. Shit, is it split?

I look towards him to see him working out harder than before, and blowing out a breath I make my way over there slowly. Todd stops me halfway and offers me a water bottle. I take it with a mumbled thanks and a weak smile. When I reach Jago's side I slump into the chair and watch him again. He flinches when he hears me, but ignores me. Is he punishing himself?

"Thanks for not taking it easy on me." His head snaps around and his eyes widen in shock. "Can you show me how to move like that?" I gush, leaning forward and wincing when I catch my lip.

He looks at my lip and frowns. "You need to get checked out by a doctor."

Well, that isn't happening. "I'm fine, will you show me?" I repeat, not giving him an out. He sighs and turns to face me again.

"Why is this so important?" he questions, searching my face for the truth.

I could spin some pretty lies but instead I give him the truth. "Because nothing down here interests me. I haven't felt that alive like I just did in years, not since I lost my parents. I want to see the world, I want to experience it, and I never want to be caught weak again. I want to be able to protect myself. I won't stop until I am a patrol and we both know without the right training I won't make it long."

He stares at me and I stare right back.

"Fuck, fine," he grunts.

I go to celebrate, and he holds his hand up. "You have one month, if at the end of it I say no, that you aren't good enough or ready, you will drop this stupid dream. If at any point during training I decide you aren't trying hard enough and good enough, I will cut you. I will treat you like any other recruit, you don't get special treatment because you are a girl," he finishes, obviously trying to scare me off.

"Thank fuck, I don't want to be treated like a delicate flower. It's not who I am, I want to be treated the same and I expect you to hand me my ass if I don't do well. I wouldn't have come to you if I wanted to be coddled."

His lips twist and his eyes drop to my lips once again. "Fine, recruit. First thing tomorrow. Five AM sharp, we will have an hour of one-on-one training to get you up to scratch as quickly as possi- ble, then you will train all day with the others. Understood?" he orders, his voice hardening.

"Yes, sir, capt, main dude," I carry on, and he groans before turning back to the weights.

"Go get your face checked recruit, that's an order." With that he dismisses me.

I nod and scamper away before he changes his mind. I get a few nods of respect on my way out and I walk with my head held high. All until I stumble into medical and spot Evan working. Fuck, isn't he supposed to be on patient required only?

I spin away ready to leave when his voice stops me cold. "Piper, what the fuck happened to your face?"

Chapter 3
Stupid Rules

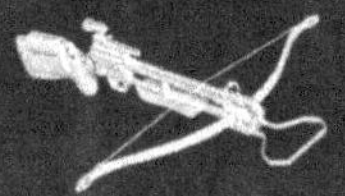

I spin around like I wasn't just trying to run away and watch as he leaves the patient he was treating to storm towards me, his face like thunder and his eyes running across me. "Funny story, you see—"

He cuts me off straight away. "Shut the fuck up and tell me who," he demands, anger lacing his words but also worry. It makes me soften towards him before I remember I'm trying to distance myself.

"I'm fine," I state and hop up on the bed. I watch as he fights himself, his jaw clenching and hands balling into fists, before he turns to me and drags the privacy curtain shut. He steps up close, until our knees touch, and glares down at me. "Tell me now, Pip."

"Why? You going to kick their ass?" I snark, hurt returning to me even as I push it away.

"You bet the fuck I am," he growls, his nostrils flaring, and I can see he is really angry, no, not angry—livid.

"No need. It was my choice," I say, looking away.

"What the fuck does that even mean Piper?" he shouts, and the curtain slides open and a nurse pokes her head around.

"Everything okay Doctor—"

He cuts her off mid-sentence. "Fine, shut the fucking curtain." She pales before throwing me a sympathetic look and shutting the curtain after her. Evan's moods are lethal and well known, and he is at the peak at the moment.

"Ev, please, my head hurts too much to argue right now," I whine, looking down at my knees and fiddling with my ring.

I hear his breathing stutter before his finger curls under my chin and lifts it. "You better tell me everything Pip, I thought we didn't have secrets from each other." I see him deflate and the hurt in his expression before he turns away, busying himself with a tray of medicines and antiseptic.

Sighing, I slip off the table and wrap my arms around him from behind. No matter my issues, they are just that, my issues, and he doesn't deserve to be hurt because of them. I know he loves me, and it must kill him seeing me like this.

"I'm sorry, I just needed some space 'kay? I promise we are good, and I am fine." He is stiff in my arms but soon melts, blowing out a breath and turning, before drawing me into a hug, careful of my aching ribs and head. I snuggle deeper, breathing in the scent that is just him. He might be a twat to everyone else, but I know deep down he is a big softie.

"Space from me?" he asks, and I can hear the sadness in his voice. I don't look up because I don't want to be the reason he is hurting.

"From everyone, I needed to think some shit through," I admit, hedging the truth.

"Did you figure it out?" he presses, and I can hear the hesitation in his voice. I nod against his chest before stepping back and slipping from his arms.

"Yep, you aren't going to like it, but you either need to be supportive or not say anything at all. Now can we be done with all this mushy shit?" I fidget and he grins at me, but I can still see the concern in his eyes. I jump back up on the table and my head spins. Evan rushes to my side and cups both sides of my face, swearing as he waits for me to breathe through it.

"I'm fine," I mumble and tap his hands, not admitting how amazing it feels for him to hold me.

"Tell me everything, and if you leave anything out, I will revoke your cuddle privileges for a month," he warns as he turns away to sort out some medical shit.

I freeze at his words, looking at the floor. I told myself I would draw a line between us, keep it friendly, but I can never sleep unless I am in his arms. I don't feel safe. Not that I told him that, he just knows I have nightmares. Knocking the problems away for another day I start from the top. When I am done, he is gaping at me.

"Seriously, you need to shut your mouth. You look like you are sucking ghost dick," I say helpfully and he snaps his mouth shut with an eye roll.

"Piper, be serious for a second. What the hell were you thinking?" He scowls at me and I wince as he dabs my cut lip.

When he's done, I reply, "It's my choice, remember what I said about being supportive? Who believed in you when you said you were going to select early and become a doctor? Who ran through all those stupid tests and medical books with you?"

He sighs and looks down, defeated. "Fine, I don't like it, but you are right. I can't exactly quiz you on this, but I will patch you up afterwards. Just promise me you will stay smart. If it gets to be too much, there is no shame in backing out."

I nod and he smiles, but it looks strained. "Seriously, you should have seen me though. I was kicking ass, taking names..." I can see he is uncomfortable, so I trail off, and it makes me sad. Is this a part of my life I am going to have to keep from him? That would cause distance and I know it.

"Kicking ass, taking names?" comes a familiar gruff voice from the curtain.

I grin and look up to Jago. "Fucking yeah I was. Not my fault you're some kind of super strong machine. Whatcha doing here, el capitan?"

He groans and leans against the wall where I can see him. I see

Evan throwing looks between us before he obviously connects the dots. He stands up and glares at Jago who completely ignores him.

"Stop calling me that recruit. I came to make sure you did as you were told for once," he replies.

"Then you obviously don't know Pip," Evan snarls, before turning around and smashing the tray of equipment about.

"Pip?" Jago snorts and looks at me. "Cause you are short?" "Pfft, I am not short. You are just massive," I defend and I can almost feel the steam rising from Evan's head.

"Yeah, I also heard that, apparently, I am hot, but a cunt?" he queries and I tilt my head, where did this playful side come from. When his eyes flicker to Evan I roll mine. Boys.

"Cummuffin actually," I point out and he inclines his head.

"See you tomorrow," he points out before straightening and turning to leave.

"Yup, five AM el capitano!" I shout after him and I see him shake his head.

I look back at Evan to see him glaring holes in Jago. "Er, Ev? You okay?" I ask.

He turns to me, his face red and his eyes narrowed. "Fine, why?" He questions, his voice tight.

"Oh, no reason, just that you are breaking your medical thingies." I jump down and smile at him before leaving too.

"Fuck!" I hear him shout, and I laugh as I head back to my room to shower.

Evan and I moved out of the orphan quarters when he chose his selection. He convinced whoever is in charge of housing to give us en-suite rooms right next to each other. His, of course, is a lot larger and has a living room, that's why we tend to hang out there. Usually I would just go straight there, but I remember my promise of drawing lines. So instead, I go to my own and shower before relaxing in bed. I must fall asleep at some point, because I hear shuffling and I dart upright just as Evan climbs onto the bed. I eye him before sliding backwards wordlessly so my back hits the wall. He gets in and faces me, our heads sharing the same pillow, our pinkies wrapping around each other automatically.

I close my eyes, beyond tired as our legs tangle.

"Are you mad at me?" he whispers into the dark room, sounding so much like the little boy I grew up with.

"No Evvie. I'm not mad, I'm just realising some things," I reply, the dark making me brave.

"What things?" he asks softly, moving closer so our foreheads touch and we are sharing the same air, our lips so close.

"Things like it's time I grow up and stop chasing you," I admit, opening my eyes. I can barely see him it's so dark, but I hear his quick inhale.

"You never have to chase me, it's always me and you," he replies.

I swallow hard. "I wish that was true." Untangling my finger and legs, I turn over and face the wall as the first tear drops onto my pillow.

He's silent before he lets out a sigh, shuffling closer he curls up behind me, his arm draping over my waist and his leg thrown over mine. "You'll see," he whispers into my ear before gently kissing my neck. I hold in my gasp as he buries his head into the back of my neck and hair.

So much for my fucking rules.

Chapter 4
Pleasure Pump

Evan is gone by the time my alarm goes off at 4:30am. The lights in my room come on automatically with the noise. When my hand falls to his spot I can feel it is still warm and it sends a tingle through my body that I choose to ignore. Sluggishly, I get to my feet and get dressed in workout clothes. Looking up I notice the clock—shit, I won't have time to get coffee.

I debate what would be worse, today without coffee or facing Jago being late. It's a hard battle but eventually I trudge to the gym, ignoring my soul reaching for that dark caffeinated goodness.

I get there just in time to see him unlocking the door and slipping inside. Grumbling, I follow after him and slide in before the door shuts.

"Mornin' captain," I say tiredly. He spins and glares at me. "Fuck, don't sneak up on me." He takes one look at me and rolls his eyes. "Come on, a good workout will wake you up."

The days pass in a blur of training and more training. I see less and less of Evan, only at night when he slips into my bed when he thinks I am asleep. Instead, I spend all my days with Jago. On the fifth morning of me running late again, which has been every day with no caffeine, I turn up at the gym. Without a word, he thrusts a cup at me and walks to set up the gym. Peering down I spot coffee. Praise the gods.

"I knew you liked me," I say before taking a sip and sighing in happiness.

"Don't push it," he grumbles, as he lifts the three mats and carries them to the middle of the floor. I watch his muscles as he heaves the mats which, when I tried to pick up I couldn't even budge, with no effort and drops them in place without breaking a sweat. I find myself checking him out pretty much all the time. It's hard to ignore the tingles in my body, or how my heart speeds up. Or my vagina turning into a slip n slide whenever he's around, something I saw on a film with Evan, especially when he is pinning me or teaching me a move which means him maneuvering me. I am a total perv, and I am cool with that.

But he does push me harder, every day I feel myself getting stronger and the moves come easier. He drills me—hehe—hard, like he promised, not giving me any special attention. After our own training session each morning, I spend five hours with the other recruits learning hand-to-hand, defence, different forms of fighting, and how to kill a person. It's intense and three men have already dropped out. Jago eyes me every day like he expects me to quit, and every day I come back harder and more raring to go. Every time I nail a move, I see the pride flash in his eyes before he covers it. I will admit it sends a thrill through me.

I spot the other recruits eyeing us both, but I ignore the looks and keep pushing myself harder. I will prove them all wrong, Evan too.

Downing the cup, I put it on the side and start to stretch like Jago taught me. As I bend down, I feel someone behind me before hands grip my hips, the heat of them burning through and branding me.

"You need to twist when you do that," Jago murmurs and twists my hips like he wants me to.

"Okay," I reply, trying to keep the breathlessness out of my voice. All this sweaty bodies touching every day thing is riling me up. I am like a walking, talking lady hard-on.

His hands linger there for a moment before he lets go and steps back. I straighten and run through the other warm ups, trying to ignore him as he circles me and points out corrections every now and then. Once I am done, he nods and kicks off his boots. I do the same and we walk onto the mats, facing each other.

"We will practice that hold we tried yesterday, I want you to be able to do it in your sleep," he says as he steps back.

I nod and get into position. With my back to him I wait, my only warning is the slight movement in the air, his feet silent on the mat, before I go down hard. Landing on my face as he pins me there, I push back with my arms and legs like he taught me but it's no use.

Eventually, I manage to get out of the position, but it took way too long. Jumping to my feet I aim my back at him. "Again, that was too slow. They aren't going to wait while I figure it out," I growl, pissed at myself.

We do the move time after time, until I can get out of it quicker each time. He drops me again, but I was expecting it. Ready to get out of it, I freeze when I feel his hardness pressed against my arse.

Panting, I wiggle back, trying to get free only to freeze when he groans. The silence stretches and I try and ignore his cock pushing against my arse.

It's like we know if we say anything or move, it will make this little bubble pop. When we hear voices coming from outside, he rolls off of me and I jump up. Ignoring me completely, he walks over to the front of the class ready to start today's lesson.

Coughing, I turn and down half my bottle of water, trying to push the feeling of his body on mine away.

My body hits the mat with a thud, again. Groaning I stand up, wincing at my poor abused ass. I wonder if Jago will massage it better? I spot him eyeing me out of the corner of my eye, so I throw him a thumbs up. He shakes his head, but I see his lips twitch, one day I will get him to fully smile. His hands are behind his back as he stalks around the mats, taking in the recruits training.

"How long have you been fucking him?" comes a sneer, and I turn to see my sparring partner eyeing my body. What was his name again, Tom? Tedd? Ryan? Some shitty name for a shitty guy. I ignore him and stretch out my arm, waiting for him to come at me again. He circles around me, his eyes blatantly perusing my body.

"I bet that's the only reason you got into this and why he went easy on you on the mat," he adds, darting in with a jab, which I block.

Panting, I dance around him and elbow his knee. He goes down, but gets up fast and whirls. "If you think Jago would go easy on anyone, whether he was fucking them or not, then you are an idiot," I say conversationally, and I see the anger flare in his eyes. In all the old books and TV shows it says getting angry makes you stupid, you miss things you shouldn't and get sloppy. Letting your rage guide you. I asked Jago once and he told me his rage constantly guides him. It's what makes him hit harder, move faster and get back up when he shouldn't be able to, but this recruit is the total opposite. He doesn't let it make him better, he uses it like a weapon. Let's it take over.

That will work in my favor, and if I can get him really angry, he might slip up. "You are just jealous that no one has ever touched your pleasure pump," I taunt and his face starts to turn red. "I am betting you sit touching it at a night, imagining you were a great warrior like Jago."

He yells and jumps forward, his arms whirring but sloppy. Grinning, I jump towards him.

Our fight turns real, each trying to land a blow. I can feel the bruising already on my body and I know he isn't pulling his punches...good. But he is nothing compared to Jago, and I have been sparring with him for five days now. He beats my ass every day, so I am used to it.

I manage to get the upper hand and he ends up on his back with me on top. He reaches his hands up high, over me and brings his fists down hard on my stomach. Again, and again, and I hold on still. Wanting to win, wanting to prove myself. They will never trust me with their backs out there unless they know I can handle myself, and I know I will have to prove myself more than the others.

"Enough!" comes a roar and I break away, turning to face Jago where he stands next to our mat. He looks furious, his face is red, and his mouth twisted in a snarl, every muscle is tight like he is ready to pounce. His eyes are spitting fire and I am pretty sure I can feel him from here. Standing there like that, he's a scary mother- fucker. The other recruits actually step away, eyeing him worriedly.

The one I was fighting cowers before him....me? I jump up and smile his way. "Sure thing, captain."

He growls, glaring at me, but when the other recruit gets to his feet Jago's anger turns on him. "You ever, and I mean ever, disobey an order again and I will kill you myself." His voice is cold and hard, every word pushed out of clenched teeth.

The recruit nods, his face pale as his body shakes, but it sends a perverse pleasure through me when I spot his nose bleeding.

"Do you understand me?" Jago snarls, stepping until they are toe-to-toe. Side by side the difference is staggering. He's massive, a fucking beast, but it's the power he wears that makes other men want to piss themselves. I wonder what that power would feel like between my thighs. Shit, okay. Bad Piper. Think of other things than his Moby Dick.

When the recruit nods, gulping like he might be sick, Jago turns his attention back to me. His eyes rooting me to the spot even as I smile at him. He doesn't scare me. His eyebrow raises when he sees I am just waiting for him, but he steps up close to me like he did the other recruit.

"Do you understand me?" he asks again, but I can see the anger in his eyes has lessened and what looks like...amusement, dances in their fiery depths.

I nod and smile at him, my shit-eating grin as Evan calls it. He snorts as I fake salute him. "Aye, aye, Captain. Sir, yes sir."

"What did he say to you?" he says, his voice lowered and velvety.

Only for my ears.

Tilting my head, I eye him, smirking all the time. "Maybe I just didn't like his face."

He huffs and steps back, his face wiping clear of his amusement as he turns towards the waiting recruits. "These two will run laps until they can't move. The rest of you are dismissed, don't forget tomorrow I will be testing you. Three of you will get to go on patrol with the other guards for one night, or more if you do well." With that, he turns to eye us with an expectant expression. I salute him once again and start to jog around the room. The other recruit falls in behind me, making sure not to get too close.

I concentrate on my breathing as I run, ignoring everything else until I circle the room and see the other recruit stumbling to his ass in the middle. Jago eyes him with a disapproving frown. He barks something at him and the other recruit stumbles from the room on jelly legs. I know the feeling, every step I take sends agony through my muscles and they feel like they are about to give out from under me.

"You can stop running," Jago shouts, watching me curiously. "You-said-not-until-we-fell-down," I pant, but my stride is slowing.

"Piper, stop," he sighs and I slow down into a stop, bending over to catch my breath before I drag my exhausted ass to the mats and collapse on my back.

"Evil. You are evil," I declare, pointing my finger into the air before it drops back down to my chest with a thump.

I hear him snort again. Hot, big hands grip one of my thighs as he digs his fingers in, making me moan long and loud. "Fuck," I say and he grunts again.

I let him work in silence, massaging all my aches and soreness away until I am a turned on, sweaty mess and he only touches me with his hands. "Where did you come from?" I blurt and almost smack myself in the face. "I mean like, I know you came from a vagina, but you weren't born down here..." I trail off when I notice he isn't moving his hands anymore. They are just gripping my upper thigh.

"Does it matter?" he asks eventually, starting to massage me again.

"No, not to me. I am just curious," I admit, tilting my head so I can see him. He doesn't look my way but concentrates on his hands touching me, his face turned away from me.

"You don't want to know," he answers eventually, his dark voice making me shiver, but it doesn't stop me from leaning up onto my arms, watching him.

"You were born out there, weren't you?" When he doesn't answer I carry on, "What happened to your parents, what is it like out there?"

He spins on me, his hand spanning to the mat on either side of me, and his face is dark and dangerous. "You want to know what it's like out there? It's a fucking nightmare. Everything is a fight for survival. Against the sun, the heat. Against the land itself, and don't get me started on the people. I see the stars in your eyes, you dream of the world out there, but it will only disappoint you just like everyone else. It's nothing but dust and death and you won't survive."

I look into his eyes and watch the trust in them, he really does believe that. It makes me sad for him, that he can't rely on anyone, that he has no one. I reach out and lay my hand on his chest. I can feel his heart racing against my palm, and I lower my voice, making it soft and calm. "Then teach me, teach me to survive. Watch my back and I will watch yours."

He snorts again, but it sounds self-loathing more than anything. "Why would I do that? Why would I trust you, when I don't even know you?"

"Then get to know me. You really just going to keep on fighting everyone and everything, every moment of the day? All I am asking is for you to give me a chance, I am doing everything you ask. I am working harder than anyone else. Tell me you don't see me improving. I am not saying we need to braid each other's hair and talk dick to rim, but a partnership."

We stay like that, with my hand on his chest, and I watch the fight in his eyes. "I told you I would train you. At the end of the month if you don't make the cut, that is your own fault. If you do, I will take you out on a patrol. Better me than one of those idiots," he mutters the last, as if almost to himself, but I smile.

"Sounds good, captain."

He shakes his head. "Stop calling me that," he grunts and leans back, letting my hand drop, and moves onto my other leg.

"Boss man? Beast? Stud muffin?" I wiggle my eyebrows and he snorts again, and I see his lips curve into a smile.

"Aha! I saw that, so you do smile! Muffin it is!" I point and grin, and he glares at me again.

"Don't you dare," he warns in the same voice he used on the recruits earlier, but it just makes me giggle.

"What's wrong, muffin?" I yelp when he smacks my thigh. "What's wrong, princess, scared of a little pain?" he mocks and I laugh again.

"Only if it doesn't come with a hot guy." I wink and he shakes his head and leans back, sitting next to me.

"What's the deal with you and the doctor?" he asks, out of the blue.

Sitting up I cross my legs with a wince, and he looks way too happy at my pain. Sadistic man. "Why?" I drawl, dragging the word out.

"Never mind," he grunts, grabbing two bottles of water and throwing one at me. I grin and take a swig, my eyes still on him.

"Aww, muffin, is you jealous?" I question all cutesy.

He glares at me and I grin back. "Not a chance, princess. Just wondering if he is going to come storming in here again and try to kick my ass."

I snap upright, eyeing him, all teasing disappearing. "He threatened you? Evvie? The guy who avoids touching other people because he hates them?"

Jago leans back with a nod. "It seems he doesn't like the fact I am 'encouraging your delusions,'" he explains, and my chest freezes before anger bursts to life. "He said if I didn't stop training you, we would have a problem."

Blowing out a breath, I grind my teeth. "Did you hurt him?" Because no one, and I mean no one, would get away with threatening the Beast and not end up hurt.

"Do you want me to?" he asks seriously.

I honestly think about it, so hurt that he would say that and go behind my back. "No, I'll do it myself." Getting to my feet I turn without another word.

"He cares, that's why he did it. I can tell that much."

I nod but don't turn around, anger racing through my veins. "Must be nice," I hear him murmur, but I am already out of the door.

Chapter 5
Deadly

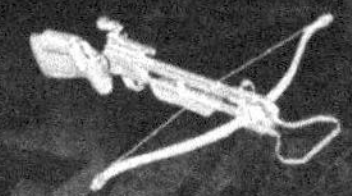

I fume for the next two hours. I went straight to Med Bay, but of course, he wasn't there. How dare he? All I asked is that he support me in the same way I did him! Yet he can't even do that. The fact that he went behind my back and threatened the man who has given me a chance, who is training and trusting me to learn just like the other recruits, infuriates me. He is such a hypocrite and the chasm between us only grows, filled with anger, betrayal, and all our unspoken feelings. It's strange how I like two very different men. Where Evan is smart, calculated, and calm. Jago is all wild fury, he's smart but he trusts in himself, he's closed off. Where Evan is a quiet thought, Jago is a storm. A force to be reckoned with.

With nothing else to do, I go back to my room and shower. Scrubbing at my skin to wash away the feeling of betrayal. When my skin turns pink, I decide to get out and towel off, but underneath I am still furious, like one word or thing might make me flip.

With the towel still wrapped around me, I walk into my room to see Evan waiting for me. He looks tired. His hair is a mess and his eyes have huge bags under them, his face is pale and concerned. It deflates me a bit but then I remember how Jago described what he said, and that white-hot anger flashes through me once again.

"How dare you?" I shout, the words tumbling from my mouth.

He must have been in his own world because he jumps and snaps his head around to face me. When he spots me in the towel, his eyes go wide and he licks his lips. Any other time and I would have been all over that, but not today.

"Huh?" he asks, his eyes locked on my legs.

"You heard me! For fuck's sake Evan, to go behind my back like that? You thought it would work? Just get me kicked out of training, completely ignoring what I wanted?" I scream the last and he walks towards me slowly.

"Pip, I just wanted what's best for you. I don't want to see you get hurt," he says sadly, locking his puppy dog eyes on me.

"Don't you fucking dare. The only person who hurt me is you. You are supposed to support me, and it doesn't matter if you think this a stupid fucking decision. You support it!" I scream as tears start to drip from my eyes.

"Pip—" He begins, stepping forward as if to hug me.

"Don't," I warn, stumbling away from him. "You hurt me more than anyone else out there ever could. This was my choice Evan, mine. I spent years supporting you, always at your back, defending you to others. We promised each other that's how it would always be, but when I need you the most, you can't get out of your own brain long enough to see that your opinion isn't needed. That I need to do this, and by going behind my back you broke my trust." I get it all out, all my hurt and anger, everything that has been building in me since I saw him with that other woman.

"Pip, I am so sorry," he cries and his eyes fill, tears slowly dripping down his cheeks. He looks heartbroken. I know the feeling.

"Don't call me that ever again. We are not family, we are not friends. I am nothing to you. How could I be? Just please, get out," I finish, my heart hurting and my chest tight. If he doesn't leave now, if he tries to hug me, I will break down. Yet, at the same time, something in me is screaming at him to push through this, to see how hurt I am, and make it better.

"Okay, I will let you calm down then we can discuss this." He wipes his eyes and turns, leaving without another word. I stagger backwards and land hard on the bed, my eyes locked on the door like he will come back. Like he will realise that I need him, now more than ever. I need his words, I need him to tell me he loves me, that he supports me no matter what. Yet he doesn't and my heart shatters.

Sobs burst from my throat as I curl into a ball, it feels like I can't get enough air and pain runs through my whole body. We have had fights before, of course we have, but none like this. None where the other one just walks away, it felt so...final, and with it, that last piece of the child inside me hiding behind his legs crumbles into dust.

I lie like that for a while, crying out my heartbreak until I can't cry anymore. My nose is stuffy and my eyes hurt, but I get up and splash some water on my face, not looking into the mirror, not wanting to see the mess I am. I can't believe he didn't come back. Do I really mean that little to him? I know he always runs from a fight, but not like that.

A knock on my door jars me out of my thoughts and I lean my head out of the bathroom, listening. It's not him, he would have just let himself in. Unless he is trying to make up and respect my privacy? The thought gets me moving until I swing the door open and see Jago waiting on the other side, looking uncomfortable as he shifts from side to side.

My heart drops again. He opens his mouth but then he really looks at me, and I see his eyes flare and his fists clench. "Who do I need to kill?" he growls, and I snort, which turns into a desperate sounding sob again, ripping through my throat.

His eyes fly wide as I rush forward and push my face into his chest, seeking comfort from the only other person I trust. I can feel him physically hesitate, obviously unsure how to deal with a crying female.

He pats my back awkwardly. "Er- There, there?" he soothes,

ending it on a question, and I can't help the snort of laughter that escapes me.

Pulling back, I see the panic in his eyes and it makes me laugh harder. He frowns at me, searching my face. "I don't do...crying," he says gruffly and I nod.

"I can see that, muffin."

He groans at the name but lets me get away with it, though I know he will punish me for it in training tomorrow. I turn and slide back into my room before falling back on the bed, making sure to clutch the towel to me. No need to give him a heart attack. I hear him shuffle before the bed dips, and I am rolled towards him. I stop myself with a hand on his steal thigh.

"What happened?" he asks, looking down at me. Sighing, I flip over until I face the ceiling.

"Don't worry about it." I lift my hand to my chest and spin my mum's ring nervously.

"Tell me, I'll kick their ass."

My lips twitch, but I don't reply until his hand cups mine, stilling my nervous movements.

"Piper, you don't have to tell me if you don't want to, but I know something that might help."

I turn my back to him, and he looks down at me softly. His hand reaches out and he moves the wet strands of my hair away from my face, the move so similar to Evan that I swallow hard.

"What's that?" I inquire, my voice shivering.

"Get dressed, princess, and I will meet you outside in five. That's an order." He stands and makes his way towards the door.

"Aye, aye captain," I call and I hear him huff a laugh.

I dress quickly and when I come out, he is leaning against the wall waiting for me. Without a word, he turns and I follow him down the hall. When we reach the gym I laugh.

"Really?" I ask, as he pushes in and I spot that it's empty at this time of night.

"It helps, trust me," he answers.

Shrugging, I follow him in as he kicks off his shoes and jacket, and moves to the middle of the mat. I do as he did and mirror him. "Hit me, get all your anger and frustration out. When you do, you will feel better."

"So, you want me to fight out my feelings?" I ask, grinning at him.

"Pretty much, just do as I said, princess," he drawls, grunting the last before holding his hands up again. Obviously done with talking. That's fine, I feel too raw and numb to try and hold a conversation.

Watching him carefully, I decide what the hell. I punch him and he catches my fist and pushes it back towards me. "Harder," he demands.

"That's what she said," I joke.

He ignores me and holds his hand up again.

I punch, time and time again, letting loose, letting my emotions guide me as I hit harder and harder. Eventually he stops catching my fists and lets me pummel his palms. "Good, keep going," he encourages as I breathe deeply.

I let loose, letting that final piece that was holding me back go until I am screaming as I kick and punch. He just stands there through it all, my rock as he lets me beat him.

I start to slow, my movements losing their fluidity and when I punch again, he catches my arm and drags me to him. I try to fight him but he's too strong. I stumble into his chest with an 'oomph.' He wraps his arms around me and holds me there, and I relax into his embrace. He doesn't talk, just lets me find comfort in his arms. It only confuses me more. For someone who claims not to trust or feel, he sure knows a lot about dealing with emotions, and here he is holding me tight like I mean something to him.

I pull myself away slightly and look up into his eyes. He looks down and I see them flare as he takes in my expression. He's beautiful. He really is, in a deadly, I will tear you into pieces if you annoy me sort of way. Even if he grunts more than speaks and disrespects my coffee gods.

He reaches up and cups my face, his hand so big that it covers nearly half of it, but he is gentle. So, opposed to when we fight, in this moment he treats me like I am precious. There are no lewd words and bumbling or wandering hands. He just watches me, waiting for whatever I will do, and I realise that for all his strength and anger there is something underneath there too, something I recognize in myself nearly every day. The need to be held, like a lost kid looking for someone in this world.

It's that thought, and the need to see if his lips are as soft as they look, that has me leaning up on my tiptoes and balancing on his chest. I can't reach him, he is that tall, so I have to wait to see if he will bend down, and I hold my breath the entire time.

Slowly, as if afraid to spook me, he leans down, bending his head until our lips touch, but he doesn't move after that and I smile against them. For someone whose nickname is Beast, he sure is gentle. He obviously feels it and starts to move back, but I reach up and thread my fingers through his hair, pulling him closer and moving my lips against his. He's hesitant at first, each touch soft and unsure, but when I bite his lower lip he groans, and his hands move down to my arse and yanks me to him. He takes control then. Holding me against his body as he demands entrance at my lips. When I open for him, he sweeps in and tangles his tongue with mine, hard, so hard and heavy, just like I imagined.

I can't help the moan that slips out. I want to climb him, so I can get closer and nothing else is between us. He obviously has the same thought, because with no effort he lifts me from the floor and I quickly wrap my legs around his waist, pushing my center right over his rock hard bulge in his sweats.

I moan again and the sound seems to drive him wild. He rubs against me as he devours my mouth, his kiss unlike any other I have ever had. Tunnelling my hands in his hair I pull away to breathe, and he tilts my head to the side and starts kissing down my neck, groaning as he does. It's the sexiest sound I have ever heard and drives me wild, making me buck against him as he sucks and licks along my neck.

The sound of the door moving has us breaking away. He drops me to my feet and I turn with a lust-filled head. When I spot no one there, I blow out a breath. What was I thinking? Anyone could have walked in and caught us, and then it wouldn't have exactly helped my case. Oh, that's right, I was thinking about what it would feel like to have all that power aimed at me.

"We should get you back," he says from behind me, his voice rough and full of desire. It makes me squirm and rub my thighs together to try and fight how bloody wet I am...and just from a kiss!

I nod without looking at him as disappointment curls in my chest. I start to walk away and I hear his footsteps behind me, just as I am reaching out for the door handle a hand lands on it, stopping me from opening it.

"Fuck it," I hear him whisper before I am spun around and slammed back into the door, his lips on mine.

I groan into his mouth as he devours me. As fast as the kiss started it ends, and by the time I blink open my eyes, he's gone. Slipping out of the gym door, he left me there with wet panties and swollen lips. Jago might be deadly to everyone else, but he is also deadly to my heart...and vagina. Definitely vagina.

Chapter 6
Scream My Name

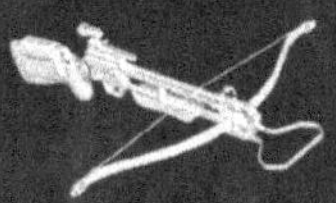

I sleep like shit that night. I keep expecting Evan to slip in and cuddle me, but when he doesn't, all the nightmares creep back. I am already up way before my alarm and decide to head to the gym—fuck, I never thought I would say that—to burn off steam.

I go through my warm-ups and decide to jog around the gym until Jago turns up. When he spots me, he raises his eyebrow but I keep jogging, lost in the moment. The rhythmic sound of my shoes slapping the cold floor is calming, letting me work through my thoughts. I don't even hear him until I look over and spot him jogging next to me. He is quiet and his face is clear for once. I hide my smile by turning back to the front, enjoying his silent support and the feeling of him next to me. Thirty minutes later, I slow to a stop and grab a drink, not wanting to wear myself out before training. I hear Jago doing the same behind me, but I take the moment to control myself, seeing him all sweaty and half naked isn't good for my sanity, or panties. Getting myself under control I turn around with my bottle raised to my mouth, only to find Jago's eyes locked where my ass was. Arching my eyebrow, I grin when his eyes snap up. He busies himself by taking a drink, but doesn't apologize for checking me out.

"Like what you see, captaino?" I tease, screwing my lid on my drink and waiting.

He swallows his water and I watch as his throat works. Fuck, why is that so hot? He lowers the bottle slowly and runs his eyes over me again. I heat up as they trace across my skin and shiver from the intensity. Fucking hell, my panties are officially done, wetter than a dog in heat.

"I like it better when it's pushed up against my cock," he admits, not the least bit ashamed. My mouth goes dry and my heart starts to race, but I can't stop the smirk crawling across my face.

"Was that your cock? Huh, I thought your nickname was Beast," I quip.

His eyes slowly reach my face and I gulp. His eyes locked on mine, he starts to prowl towards me. Grinning, I back up, turning so my back is to the room. He follows me, stalking me across the mats until I trip over the edge with a yelp. I end up on my ass and he lands over me on all fours, an inch of air between our bodies. Delib- erately, he drops his hips into mine, letting me feel his cock hard- ening in his pants. "You were saying?"

"I don't know, I might need more evidence," I say through my smile, but my voice is breathless. When we are training, I can ignore the insane attraction between us, but like this, his eyes sparkling and teasing, his hard uncompromising body pushing up against mine, I am gone. He's hot when he is in leader mode, his eyes hard and unfor- giving and his body a weapon, but pushed between my spread thighs with his head lowered to mine, passion flaring and his lips curling into that private smile...

"What, you worried Beast?" I taunt, and his lips lower until they brush mine.

"You talk too much," he growls before kissing me gently, the butterfly touch so at odds with his dangerous tone and body. All that power and he treats me like I am glass. It's cute but I need more. I can take more, I don't want him treating me with kid gloves.

Deciding to take action, I hike my legs up and wrap them around his hips, my heels resting on his ass. Using that leverage I pull him to me and reach up, twining my fingers into his hair, yanking his head to me.

He groans into my mouth and I sweep my tongue inside, tangling with his as we fight for dominance. It's not hard and hot like our kiss yesterday, this is a battle. It's like our training, each seeking the other's weakness and fighting back hard, not giving in.

He thrusts against me, his hips smacking into mine, making me groan into his mouth. I let my hands wander across every inch of exposed skin, trailing them down his back which makes him shiver against me, knowing I effect this big, scary warrior has me losing control. Gripping his shoulders, I let him feel my nails and he grunts again.

Pulling away to breathe, he nudges my face to the side, exposing my neck. Facing the door to the gym, I close my eyes in bliss and arch into his hard body as he leaves open-mouthed kisses along my neck, before sweeping back up and trailing stinging bites down it. Panting, I moan with each one, loving the sting of pain that turns into pleasure as he kisses it better.

"Jago," I moan, rubbing my hard nipples, hidden under my shirt, against his chest, needing to be skin on skin. He must feel the same because he breaks away and rips my shirt over my head before diving back in, his head lowering as his kisses cover my shoulder. Looking down at him hovering over my body, I groan. Shit, he looks like a wet dream. All chiselled muscle and perfect, his back rippling as he moves, worshipping my body.

Gripping his hair again I tilt his face up to mine to see his features contorted in pleasure and need, my chest heaving with my pants, and I can't help but drink in the sight of him. He arches his eyebrow at me and I grin, before pulling his head to where I need him, not the least bit shy in controlling him. When he relents, the feeling of having this man, this beast, under my control has my pussy clenching and arching into him.

He gets my hint and nudges up my sports bra, and I can't look away as his eyes connect with mine the same time his lips wrap around my pert nipple. Biting my lip, I try to hold in my moan. He must see the challenge in my eyes as he drags his mouth away. "I wonder if I can make you scream, put that mouth of yours to good use," he rumbles against my chest, making my eyes widen before narrowing on him.

"You wish, don't give yourself too much credit, Beast," I taunt and he grins, taking my breath away. I've seen all those little smiles and his lips quirking, but this cocky, sure as shit smile has me wanting to jump him. It lights up his whole face and tightens my body, making naughty thoughts run through my head.

"You know what they say about beasts right?" he murmurs, nipping my nipple and making me grit my teeth, determined to stay quiet. "They make you scream." With that, he wraps his lips around my nipple and sucks as he ravishes me.

My usual in control, serious warrior is fracturing to show the animal underneath, and he is all passion and sex, so in contrast to how I imagined him. It's a new side of him, the teasing, the playfulness, and I find both of them sexy as fuck. The warrior who commands me, and the beast who drags me to the edge of pain and pleasure.

He rips off my sports bra and it joins my shirt on the floor behind us, and he takes turns switching from nipples, his fingers wrapping around the one not in his hot, wet mouth. Tweaking and plucking until I am writhing underneath him, but I need more. I don't even have to ask, it's like he can sense it. His hand wanders away from my breast and explores me, dipping into my curves and spanning my waist. Looking down at the size of his hand, the tanned skin against my pale flesh has me groaning, the noise slipping out before I can help it. I feel him smile against my breast as his fingers edge under the waistband of my stretchy pants, stroking the skin of my pelvis. Driving me wild. Fuck, I just know I am going to lose this bet. Men don't always like a dominant female in bed but I know Jago will, it's in his eyes whenever I answer back, or when I meet him head on. He's not used to someone standing up to him, his face dark and his eyes filled with horrors. He has been alone his whole life, but I will remind him what it feels like to lean on someone else, because two can play this game.

Tightening my legs around his waist, I flip him like he taught me and grin down at him as he stares up at me from the mat, looking shocked, but his expression soon ignites into a fire as I grind down onto him. His hands raise to my hips, and with a quick snap I grab both, banging them on the mat above his head.

His eyebrow arches but I feel his cock jerk against me. He might not admit it, but he wants someone to come in and break down those walls, push him to his limit, challenge him in all ways. I know because I feel the same way.

As I lean down, his eyes start to shut, obviously expecting me to kiss him, but instead I dart to the side and kiss down his neck like he did to me. He freezes against me and I nip gently, when he doesn't react apart from his heart rate increasing and his hands threading through mine, I bite harder. He roars and his hips jerk up to mine as I dig my teeth in, his hands raise and I know he isn't really trying, because he could lift mine if he wanted.

Letting go, I lick the bite mark gently and looking at the teeth marks in his neck and I grin, it's going to leave a bruise. He is going to have to walk around with my mark on his neck all week, the thought should not please me so much, but it does.

He groans against me, his breath fanning my cheek, and I pull farther back to see his pupils are blown and he looks slightly dazed. I don't wait for him to come back around, because I know he will get payback for that. Licking down his neck, I blow over the wet skin and he shivers against me. Kissing and licking across his chest I look up at him as I reach his nipple. I grin and his eyes narrow down at me, and keeping my gaze still locked with his, I wrap my lips around his nipple and suck. Mirroring his movements.

He groans and thrusts up, jostling me on his lap. Groaning, I grind down onto him, needing more. My panties are soaked and I can't be bothered with restraint anymore. I know we are in the gym, I know anyone could walk in, but the thought sends a bolt of lust straight down to my throbbing pussy. Pulling away slightly I flick my tongue over his nipple as my hand skates down his rock hard stomach, teasing his muscles before I slip it into the waistband of his shorts.

I freeze and he grins, holy fucking dick and balls he really is a beast. Wrapping my lips back around his nipple, I wrap my hand around his length at the same time and squeeze. He moans, thrusting up into my hand. I glide my hand up and down, feeling him. Fuck, he's big, bigger than anyone else I have been with. He's wide, but not too wide. I can feel the pre-cum covering the top of his cock and I use it to wet it, stroking him a few times as I nip at his nipple.

He growls, the rumble sending a shiver through me as my pussy throbs again. Obviously tired of my teasing, he rolls us, making me lose my grip on his cock and nipple. Lying underneath him I blink in a daze, but he doesn't wait. Switching his grip to one hand, he grabs my shirt from the mat and ties my wrists together over my head, pushing them into the mat. "Don't move them or I stop."

With that warning he crawls down my body, stopping to lick and tease both nipples before running his tongue along my stomach. Licking along my waistband, his finger slips under and without hesitation, his hand covers my panty covered pussy.

He presses hard and I rub myself against him. His hand slowly pulls out and I want to scream. Fucking hell, the bloody teasing cuntholio. What's a girl gotta do to get fingered around here? Oblivious to my inner dialogue, he grips my joggers and yanks them down, lifting my ass I let him pull them down to my feet and I kick them off until I am just in my black cotton panties. Yet he looks at me like I am a feast. His eyes devouring all my skin, burning with lust and something else. He looks at me like he has never seen anything so beautiful, hell, I know I have a good body but for once, I feel comfortable and sexy as hell.

His fingers gently caress a small scar on the top of my left thigh, one I got when Evan and me were playing hide and seek when we were younger, a small piece of metal was sticking out inside cupboard I hid in, and in the dark I didn't see it. I had slipped back, my hands covering my giggles as he walked past until I felt the shelf fall and dig into my leg. A cry had escaped and he found me, grin- ning from ear to ear until he saw the tears welling in my eyes, and the rip and blood on my trousers. He had pulled me from the cupboard, picked me up, and struggled with me back to the room before laying me on my bed. I stayed and watched as he ran around before returning to me and patching me up, once a doctor always a doctor. Pushing the thoughts of Evan away, I smile as he explores my body languidly like he has all the time in the world.

His fingers brush the birthmark on my hip before he tugs down my panties, obviously seeing the top of the black outline. Gazing down he circles the little tattoo. I wet my lips and watch his reaction, and his eyes turn understanding. "You lost them both?" he murmurs and I nod, leaning my head back to look at the ceiling. I don't want to see the pity in his expression when he takes in the two roses curling around my hip with the dates scrawled artistically through them. I had them done in secret and showed Evan after. He loved it, his hand stroked my hip before he yanked himself away and went back to work. It shouldn't matter that the thought sends more heat to my pussy, even as my heart twangs. I am so fucked up.

His fingers dance lower until he covers my bare pussy this time. We both freeze, staring at each other. We have been teasing so far but passing this step means we can't go back but I want him, I have since the moment I saw him, and it has only been growing every day until all I can think about is him. His smile, his body, this growly man has taken over me.

I arch into his hand and it's like the last of his restraints break away, leaving nothing but the beast. He kicks open my legs, leaving me open to him as he stares down at my naked wet pussy with a ravenous hunger that has me rubbing against his still hand. He opens my lips and runs his finger down me, before thrusting one inside of me with no warning. A long moan leaves my lips as I arch up, needing more. Grunting, he watches as his finger slides in and out, before he adds another and curls them inside of me, hitting that bundle of nerves.

"Jago, please," I plead, feeling needy.

"I like it when you say my name, I can't wait until you scream it," he growls before lying between my parted legs. His words finally click in my mind and I narrow my eyes ready to lay into the cocky bastard, but then his tongue flicks out and he licks me from the top of my pussy to my arse, and all thoughts and reasons leave my mind. He devours me like I am his favourite dessert, his tongue licking me clean before flicking my clit. My hands try to drift down but I end up frowning when I realise they are still bound. He grins against me before his fingers start to move again, thrusting in and pulling back slowly. I need more, I need harder. I don't realise I have even said it out loud until, with a yelp, I am rolled onto my front and my hips are yanked savagely back, my arse and pussy in the air.

My face hits the mat and I tilt it to the side so my cheek is resting there. He doesn't wait or ease in as he thrusts three fingers back into me and his mouth closes on my clit, sucking hard. I come with a scream, my pussy milking his fingers. When the pleasure finally stops and I am shaking, only his grip on my hips is holding me up and I want to groan. I bloody screamed, the cocky bastard will never let me live that down. He leans over me, his sweaty chest meeting my back as he covers me. "You didn't scream my name, I guess I will have to try again."

His voice rumbles through me as he breathes onto my neck. Shivering against him I freeze as his teeth grip my earlobe and tug. His cock is pressed against my arse cheek and I can feel his pre-cum on my skin, the thought makes me wild. I push back against him, needing him inside me.

"Fuck me and I might," I taunt and he thrusts against me, but we both freeze when we hear talking outside the gym.

"Shitasourusrex." I roll to the side, quickly shimmying out of the bindings on my hands, luckily he didn't do them to tight, and grabbing my bra. Jago jumps up and pulls up his trousers, passing mine to me. Our little bubble bursts. I quickly get dressed, feeling sticky and still needy as hell. When I am dressed and panting, he steps closer, blocking my view of the door. Leaning down he kisses me hard before saying, "We will finish this later, this whole training session I am going to be thinking of you riding my cock." With that he turns, and I quickly grab my bottle of water and down it.

Not a moment later, the recruits come into the room, a few throw us narrowed eyed looks but I grin and Jago just grunts, back to being the emotionless instructor. Hiding all that passion and intensity behind his wall.

"Warm up, I want you split into partners in the next ten minutes. It's test day, let's see who fails."

Shit, I forgot about the test. Not only am I going to have to fight these fuckers with my own cum dripping down my leg, but I also have to get tested on my moves. Fuck it, I can do it.

Chapter 7
Test Day

Giving myself a pep talk, I watch as all the other recruits stream in, the one who I attacked a couple of days ago purposely standing next to me, so close I can feel him and smell his sweat. Crinkling my nose, I stare forward, ignoring him the best I can.

"Hey, slut," he murmurs, glancing at me and then down at my body.

"Really, slut? That's the best insult you could come up with? What about assbandit, turdburglar, shitface mcgee? The list is endless, and you go with slut?" I ask, shaking my head at him in disappointment. His eyes narrow on me in anger as his cheeks heat, I guess that wasn't the reaction he was after.

"Yeah, well you are one. Think you can fuck your way to patrol, why don't you get on your knees and show me how you made it this far," he sneers, grabbing his crotch.

I mean really, why is that the go-to thing? "Why don't you get on yours sweetie, put your mouth to good use instead of talking shit?" I wink and run my eyes over him as I lick my lips.

He blinks at me in astonishment and I laugh, turning back around to see everyone looking between us. I wink at Jago and he grunts, a smile dancing on his lips before he clears his face and claps his hands.

"Shut the fuck up recruits. Today is test day. I am going to push you to your limit until you are crying in a corner pissing in your pants. The person I think did the least shittiest will be going on patrol with C Team tonight!" he shouts, stalking down the front line and making eye contact with everyone.

Two guys in front of me start nudging each other and whispering, I watch in amusement as Jago catches them and stalks towards them, towering over them when he stops toe to toe. "Feel like sharing whatever the fuck you pussies are whispering about?" he demands, eyeing them in disgust.

"N- no, sir," the one on the left stutters out, and Jago glares at them before turning and walking back to the front. I watch as the one on the right nudges him again, obviously laughing at his friend.

"First up, hand-to-hand!" Jago shouts. "Mat clear, one-on-one, wait for your name to be called." Everyone jumps into action and I stroll to the edge of the mat and sit my ass down, ready to watch him kick some ass.

"Bad Hair and Cry Baby, you are up." He points out two guys and I snigger at the nicknames, I wonder if he has one for me.

The two jump up and face each other on the mat. Jago signals for them to start, and everyone begins chanting and throwing out helpful hints as they circle each other. They look evenly matched, both are skinny and about the same height. They usually pair up as well, so they know how the other would move.

The fight is over pretty quickly, Bad Hair, as Beast calls him, darts in with a weak looking punch and they start fighting for real. Each hit is held back, you can tell they are afraid of hurting each other something, and Jago must spot that.

"Oh, I'm sorry, would you like me to give you some kid gloves and padding? Do you think the creatures out there will take it easy on you? Fucking hit each other!" he shouts, watching them, his face blank. My eyes keep getting drawn back to him. He is standing opposite me, the fighting happening between us, but he dominates my whole attention. His feet are bare, he has those joggers still on and he's shirtless. His big arms are crossed, showing off his muscles and he looks like a ruthless bastard. I glance back to the fight, but my gaze flits back to him in time to see him roll his eyes. He catches me staring at him and arches his eyebrow, amusement dancing in the fiery depths of his eyes.

Not the least bit embarrassed to be caught staring, I wink and look back at the fight. The guy with the Bad Hair lets out an embarrassing yell and punches the other in the face. The Bad Hair goes down with a squeak as the Cry Baby shakes out his hand. I cringe, really? They want to be patrol. Jago will rip them to shreds. As if my thoughts called him, he stalks to the mat and looks between the two. "Get the fuck out of my gym," he growls, and the bad haired kid grabs his friend's arm and drags him away, both of them red faced and looking over their shoulder as they leave. Jago pinches the bridge of his nose and points at two random men.

It goes like this for a while. I make sure to catalogue who did good and who did bad. I also make sure to watch their moves, to see their triggers or if they throw off signals when they are going to move. Any of it can help me and I plan to be the best.

There are only three of us left now and I am not sure how it's going to work. The guy who I faced last time gets paired up with a big bastard, but he seems confident. I had to laugh when Jago called the slimy fucker 'Eel.' I watch their fight closely, I know at some point I will have to face him again and I need to be ready. He moves fast and hits hard, he obviously knows how to fight and what his weaknesses are. The other guy is a hard hitter, but he moves too slow. The fight is over quickly, since Eel obviously comes to the same conclusion and takes him down before the big guy can land a hit.

He jumps on the spot, sweat beading on his forehead, and he smirks at me. Gritting my teeth, I watch as he struts off the mat and stops in front of me. "Room is L corridor, feel free to stop by later to fuck a real man." He steps to the side when Jago whistles.

"Good job, okay, last up is Brawler over there." Brawler, really? That's my nickname? I suppose it could have been worse. Standing slowly, I shake out my muscles from sitting too long. Looking around in confusion I open my mouth, when Jago steps on the mat and faces me with an expectant expression. Shit, really. I am so going to get my ass whooped.

Unwilling to show them my annoyance, I step onto the mat and face him, throwing him a cocky smile. I am going to go down swinging, that's for sure.

"Don't worry about landing a hit, just show me what you can do," he says loudly enough for everyone to hear, and annoyance blooms in my chest. He grins and I know he did it on purpose, he knows I will need to land a hit now and it will make me work harder. Cocky little shit, I am going to get my own back later.

He doesn't give me any warning and I know he isn't holding back anymore. In our training sessions, he takes the time to show me how to avoid a move, he doesn't hesitate to put me on my arse, but this feels like our first fight all over again. He is actively trying to attack me, and I guess I will have to react.

He goes to kick out my feet and I jump back, already swinging my fist like he taught me, my other hand coming up. He blocks both and twists my wrists. I follow with the movement and manage to break the block, darting out of hitting range.

Breathing heavily, I wait for him to move next, and he darts in. His movements are so fast I can barely see him, as he rains down punches and kicks until I'm stumbling back trying to block them, but I manage to. I know he won't slow down easily, so there is no point waiting for that. I duck under his arm and he spins to follow me, showing me his unprotected side. I punch and he grunts, making me grin as I dance backwards. I see the appreciation in his eyes even as he comes at me again. We go on like that, the room silent apart from our breathing and gasps as we land hits. I manage to land a kick on his thigh, which makes him stumble, and I quickly follow it up with a knee to his groin but he twists at the last moment, and I dart backwards as he shows me he was holding back. A kick to my thigh, mocking me, has my leg going dead, and he jabs at my middle. He grabs my arm and throws me over his head and follows me down, pinning me, but I wrap my legs around his head like he taught me and twist until I am on top.

Tightening my thighs around his neck, I grunt as he hammers into my legs with his fists. Shit, this will hurt tomorrow. I tighten my legs and he grunts, his face turning red. His legs come up and wrap around my head, his ankles locked behind me, and he drags me down to the mat. He quickly cuts off my breathing and I gasp. Fuck, he has so much more power than me.

My vision starts to dot as I struggle for breath. I enjoy choking as much as the next girl, but damn. When I just think I am about to pass out he lets go and I roll to my side, sucking in air. Motherfucker, I am so not touching his cock tonight...

"You dead, Brawler?" he asks and I can hear the amusement in his voice. Ballsacklicker.

I throw a thumbs up and I hear him snigger, before he grabs my hand and yanks me to my feet. He stands in front of me and I ignore everyone else as he gently strokes my throat. "Best get that checked, Brawler," he says softly, making the nickname sweet coming from his lips. He seems to remember everyone else is there then because he clears his throat and steps back, his face going blank once more and I realise how much emotion he just let me see. Okay, I might have to touch his cock a little bit, because even though I nearly passed out, my panties are soaked once again. Fighting with Jago really shouldn't turn me on this much. I guess Evan was right, I am weird.

"Next up is endurance," he shouts and I groan.

We spend the next hour testing our limits, we run laps until people collapse, and we use weights until people can't feel their arms. After each mini test someone is dismissed, and they go and sit on the benches at the side just watching us. We are down to ten people now and it's getting competitive.

Dropping the last weight, I bend over with my jelly arms and pant.

"Next up, problem-solving," Jago yells and I flip him off.

He truly is evil, he seems to be getting off on watching us all struggle. The others groan as we all make our way back to the mats, where we see that while we were busy he set up some obstacles.

Luckily, I am the last to go again, and I watch as they try to figure out the problems, taking note on what doesn't work and what does. One of them is a removable wall that you have to move to get around, but you can't touch it. That one is easy, but nobody seems to notice. The next is a net on the ground, which you can't touch, again easy. The last is harder. Blocks and obstacles are set everywhere in the space with some guards patrolling. We have to use the cover and not get spotted before reaching the flag at the other end. When my turn is up, I grunt, I need to beat the time or I am fucked. I sucked at strength and was okay at endurance, so I need to be smarter.

When he tells me to start I sprint to the wall, even as the other recruits laugh, and press the button that retracts into the wall. Not waiting to see, knowing I am right, I swerve around it and lay down, before wiggling under the net, my smaller stature coming in handy here. I hear the others moaning as I face the last obstacle. The men move around, pretending that they can't see me. Looking around I form a plan. I need to get past them without being seen, which means I need a distraction.

Ducking behind a low training block, I wait until they walk past as their back is to me. Grabbing the wooden slat from the top of the box I chuck it, and when it bangs down on the floor near them they jump, and look around that side of the course. I don't waste any time pushing off and sprinting behind the next obstacle, having to go through the opening to it.

When I get there, I quickly look around the corner to see them heading my way. Shit. I can't go around this and they are coming right at me. Banging my head back I look at the ceiling while I think, suddenly I grin. Turning, I tuck my fingers into the cracks on the block and start to climb. I reach the top as quickly as I can and lay down just as they round it, and look around. I listen carefully, and when I hear their boots tapping away I roll over and look over the side. One has stopped in front of the obstacle I am laying on, while the other prowls the other side of the course. Shit. Looking round I spot the last obstacle before I can reach the flag. I won't make it if I climb down, since I will have to round the front to get around it and they will spot me and it's game over. Unless...

It's stupid and might get me hurt, but it just might work. I silently get to my knees and into a crouching position, freezing when I see the guy move but he doesn't look at me. Judging the distance between the boxes I take a deep breath and I push off using my toes. I land on the top with a thump and almost roll off the side. It's probably the only thing that stops me from being noticed because I hear the other guy move to investigate as I am hanging off the side of the box, closest to the flag. I listen hard, and I can hear them murmuring from the other side of the box. It's now or never. I fling myself backwards and roll to my feet, sprinting as quietly as I can to the flag. I grab it just as they round the box to check the other side.

I hear the recruits clap, only three people managed to get to the flag and I was one of them. Whooping, I jump up and down. When I glance to the side, I see Jago's eyes have heated with desire, and I grin before I meet the gaze of the slimy recruit who I am totally just going to call eel eyes. He is glaring at me, time for some payback.

Sauntering his way I hand him the flag. "Don't worry, I won't leave you behind out there."

I swagger away to get a drink as I hear him cursing, and the other recruits laughing and whistling. They gather round me congratulating me and talking as Jago calls a break to clean up the gym. It seems I have earned some respect today, hard won, but worth it.

We shut up when Jago steps into the middle of the room, commanding everyone's attention without even uttering a word.

"Results are in, two of you are tied so I will be sending you both on patrol." He looks everyone over, they are all worse for the wear but seem excited. "Brawler and Eel," he shouts and I groan, of course it's the arsehole. He steps forward and winks at me.

"Dismissed, both of you meet in the door bay at seven PM." With that, Jago strides away and starts packing away equipment.

Everyone jokes and laughs, congratulating me and Eel and feeling sorry for themselves as they leave, but I hang back, packing up my bag so no one questions me. When it's just Jago and me, I trot to the mats and sit my tired ass down. He glances over his shoulder as he picks up two punching bags, I watch the muscles play in his shoulders and back as he takes them to the storeroom and packs them away. When he is done, he walks towards me and grace- fully sits opposite me. Sitting on the mat, I sip my water as he watches me.

"I will teach you how to spot someone's weakness, even your own. It will help you understand them and then you can use that against them." His words have me blinking in confusion, most people would make small talk, but not Jago.

"What if they don't have one?" I ask, spinning my ring.

He turns to me, his face blank and cold. "Everyone has a weakness."

I tilt my head, considering him. "Even you?"

He breathes deep, his sweaty chest moving and drawing my eyes. He is like a predator. So still, but can burst into movement at any time. He's unpredictable, he's angry, and he's deadly. Yet I can't seem to stop the fire that is burning in my belly for him. He does things to me. His confidence, and when I see him stalking across the mats, knowing he could kill anyone who got in his way... Yep.

I have serious lady blue balls, like he got me off earlier but I just keep wondering if we would have fucked if we didn't hear them approaching. Looking at him now, as he tries to keep his eyes on my face, I think we would have. It seems Beast wants me as much as I want him.

"What should I expect from tonight?" I ask, excited but also a little bit nervous about the thought of going on patrol.

He shrugs and leans back onto his arms. "It's hard to explain, but you will not be going out with the normal patrol."

Tilting my head I watch him closely. "Why? That's what you promised the recruit..." I start to get mad, is he seriously going to take it back? Why, because I am a woman? I am just riling myself up when he cuts through the chaos in my head.

"You will be going with me," he says it like that explains every-thing, and I am just left staring at him stupidly.

"With you? I thought you worked alone?" I question curiously, even as a smile dances on my lips.

He just grunts and I have to bite my lip to hold in my smile.

"Don't trust me to behave?" I tease and I can see his lips turn up in a smile.

"That too."

Bloody man, sometimes he speaks less than Evan. Crawling closer I nudge his legs but his hand darts out and catches my foot before I can kick him again, and he holds it to him. Huffing, I lean back and stare at the ceiling. "You really not going to tell me? Is it because you don't think I can do it, or is it because I am a woman?" I ask, my words like a whip.

"Shut the fuck up, I don't give a shit if you are a woman and I do trust you." He blows out a breath and his hand clenches around my foot. "It's them I don't trust," he mutters, and I open my mouth to ask more questions when he lets go and jumps up.

"I have some shit to do. Meet me at the bunker door at seven sharp," he demands, gathering his stuff. Blinking at his change in mood I just nod, and then he is gone. Men.

I vagina up and go and get my med check, knowing Jago won't let me go if I don't. I linger outside the corridor before knocking on the door. I hear him swear before he swings it open, anger on his face when he freezes and stares at me. He just stares and I do the same. He looks tired, there are bags under his eyes, and his face is tight. His hair is more of a mess than normal, and stains cover his shirt and medical coat. It looks like he has been sleeping here.

"Are you going to let me in or just stare?" I tease, so used to our banter. He swallows hard and steps back to let me in, but he doesn't speak.

Walking past him I take in the mess that is his office. He doesn't tend to see people in here but damn. Food and lots of recycled cups are littered around his desk, and I crinkle my nose at the smell. He hurries past and his cheeks turn red as he tries to throw some of it into the bin. Okay, this is awkward, and it only makes me sad. We never struggled to talk before, hell, we were inseparable and one fight has changed that. He won't even look at me, hasn't said a word to me, and I can see this is hurting him as much as it is me.

"Evvie," I say softly and he hunches his shoulders. Okay, looks like I need to be the bigger person here. I touch his back softly and he turns around to face me, his face looks like he is waiting for a bomb to drop.

"I don't want to fight, I came to see how you are." I don't mention the med check up yet just so he doesn't think I am using him. He looks down and I drop my hand before he grabs it and holds it to his chest.

"How do you think I am?" he mutters, staring at our joined hands. "I miss you Pip."

It shatters my heart at the pain and vulnerability in his voice. "I miss you to Evvie."

He looks up and searches my eyes. "Do you?"

I tilt my head in confusion. "Of course I do, why would you even ask that?"

He looks back down again. "No reason," he mumbles, but I let go of his hand and raise his chin.

"Nope, we don't do that. We don't lie to each other," I remind, begging him to talk to me so maybe we can sort this out. He obviously feels as rotten as I do.

"Just that, I saw you and you didn't seem to be missing me." His eyes lower to the floor and I blow out a breath.

"Evan, look at me," I demand, channelling my inner Jago. When he raises his eyes I cup his face. "Never doubt how I feel about you, you are my everything, I am lost without you, of course I missed you." I search his eyes, imploring him to realise what I am saying.

"I just don't want you to get hurt," he whispers, and I see the pain and truth in his eyes, no matter what stupid things we say or throw at each other, this is what it boils down to.

"I know, but you have to realise this is what I want to do. You just need to support me." He yanks his face away and runs his hand through his hair.

"I can't, I just can't Pip," he grumbles, begging me with his eyes to understand. Anger bursts to life in my chest, he isn't even giving me the benefit of the doubt or listening to me. Does he really think I would be that stupid with my own life? I am not a child living in the clouds. I know how dangerous it is. Not wanting to start a fight I take a deep breath.

"Just come and see me fight, you will see that I am good, and it's not like I am seeking out fights. I am going on patrol with plenty of other guards, they wouldn't let me go if they weren't sure!" I beg, trying to get him to see reason, but it was the wrong thing to say. He shuts down.

"Yes, I have seen you with the other guards," he sneers and I frown in confusion. "I came to see you, to make up, obviously you were not as bothered as I was, and I watched you fight today. You are doing this for stupid reasons and you will get yourself killed like your parents," he says, straightening his shoulders as he rips out my heart. I gasp and stumble back. I see him wince but he doesn't take it back.

"You are never going to accept this or support me, are you?" I ask sadly, seeing the truth in his eyes. He would rather sabotage our relationship.

He stares at me as I step back, the distance between us bigger than ever before. Getting my teeth, I ensure my face is blank. "Well, that's that then. I guess from now on we go on as polite strangers. I will stop telling you about my life and you do the same."

I see the tears gathering in his eyes but he nods. "I think that's for the best if you are dead set on destroying yourself."

It's like another blow to my already hurting heart. I can't take much more. "Goodbye, Evvie." I turn around and walk away before I do something stupid like forgive him. We are just too different. I can't keep letting it slip by and he can't get his head out of his ass. Life is too short to put up with shit. Maybe one day he will regret his decision, but right now it's what is best for both of us. This time a sense of peace settles in my chest even as it hurts, at least I know I gave it another shot. I gave him a chance, and now everything is on his shoulders. I will miss him, but maybe it is for the best. I just wish my heart could accept that.

I stumble from his office in a daze, heading back to my room to shower and get ready for tonight. His words keep ringing in my head, hurting me every time.

"Hey, what's wrong sweetie?Break up with your boyfriend?" a familiar voice calls and I roll my eyes, not even looking back as I turn the corner. I spot my mistake easily, I shouldn't have ignored him and with the corridor being empty, it was a bad move.

I don't hear him until it's too late, I blame my hurting heart but in reality, I never expected him to attack me. Throw barbs, sure, but actually attack me? Nope.

Eel slams me into the wall, his arm across my throat as he grins at me. His body traps mine and I know I am not strong enough to fight him off this way so I relax into the wall and give him a calm expression.

"What's up, buttercup, forgot to beat your meat today?" I joke.

His face turns red and he adds pressure to my neck, I don't let it show, even as it hurts, knowing it will only egg him on.

"You really should talk to someone about your anger, there are things they can do, like, you know, cut of your tiny dick and make you into the woman you so clearly want to be." I laugh and he cuts off my breath, making me choke. He lets go a little bit and I suck in a much-needed breath.

"Seriously, how did you find out about my kink for choking? Did I say 'yes, Daddy,' while Beast was doing it earlier?" I taunt and his face looks like it is going to explode.

Pushing his dick into my stomach he smirks at me. "You talk too much, I can make that stop."

"Ew, are you on about killing me and fucking my body? Cause dude, that's weird." He growls and smashes my head back into the wall.

"Ow," I moan, gritting my teeth against the throbbing that instantly starts at the base of my skull.

"Seriously, what do you think is going to happen here? That I am going to let you stick your one-eyed monster in me?" I taunt.

"Shut up!" he screams, smashing my head back against the wall, again and again until I am dizzy and can't keep it upright. He grabs my chin and holds it up so I have to stare at him. Blinking hard I breathe through the bile rising in my throat. Hell, maybe I should just be sick on him. "You are so fucking annoying, thinking you are all that just because you sucked his cock to get into the programme. You have another thing coming, you won't make it one minute out there and I will make your life fucking hell." His spit rains down on my face and I scrunch my nose.

"Ew, say it, don't spray it," I gasp through the pain. If he is waiting for me to be scared he has another thing coming. Jago scares me more on a daily basis, plus, if I really needed to, I could take him.

I don't see the fist coming until it hits me, that sounds like a really bad song title. Groaning, I reach up and hold my face. I feel blood drip from my nose and I know that prick just split my lip. "Watch your back," he sneers and lets me go.

"That's impossible, you massive twatopotomus!" I shout. Fuck, that hurt.

I stumble back to my room and when I look in the mirror, I cringe. There is no way I am hiding this from Jago. Shit, I didn't get med checked, looks like I can kill two birds with one stone.

Chapter 8
Limb From Limb

I didn't answer any of the questions at med bay and luckily Evan wasn't there. A plump, older man whose name I can never remember took one look at me and rolled his eyes. After checking me over, he patched up my face the best he could and sent me on my way. I managed to grab some food and coffee before I made my way to the bunker room door hangar.

Leaning back against the wall, I watch as the patrol shifts change over. I missed the vehicles coming back, but I watch as they unload their finds and fill back up on supplies for the next patrol. I get some weird looks, but soon enough they ignore me and are laughing and joking with each other.

I can't wait to go out there, I wonder what it is like. Will it be everything I imagined, do people still live out there? Cities, are they still a thing? All the things my mum and dad showed me and told me stories about...

"Well, look who showed up," comes a snide voice, this time I ignore him, knowing he won't try anything with so many people around.

I can almost feel the moment Jago walks in, I purposely don't look at him but I feel Eel next to me straighten.

"What the fuck are you waiting for recruit, C Team, fucking move," he growls.

"Yes, sir, sorry sir," Eel says before scrambling over to C Team in the corner who are packing up and ready to leave for patrol.

"Did you go and—what the fuck happened to your face?" Jago demands, stopping in front of me, his face contorted in fury and his muscles bunched as if to attack someone.

"Well, you did nickname me Brawler right?" I laugh and he steps closer, his eyes spitting, he is that angry.

"No fucking jokes, who the fuck did that?" he demands, his cheek twitching and I think he might explode with how red he is getting.

"Why, you going to hurt them for me?" I ask. "I am going to kill them," he growls and I sigh.

"You can't, the rumours are bad enough, if you get pulled up for hurting someone because I got jumped we both know I will get kicked from the programme and you will get disciplined," I explain rationally, even as a part of me jumps at his beast side.

"I don't give a fuck, tell me." His voice is getting quieter and more deadly, and I know he means business.

"I think it's safer that I don't." I smile at him and his eyes narrow.

"I would never hurt you," he defends, making me laugh.

"I know that, I meant safer for the guy who did this." I point at my face and he glowers again.

Reaching across he runs his thumb along my split lip. "When I find out, I am going to rip them limb from limb," he says it softly, almost caringly, and the threat coupled with him touching me makes me want to climb him.

"We should get going, are we all packed?" I ask, trying to distract myself from the thought of riding him down to the floor in front of everyone.

He just grunts and pulls his thumb back, licking the blood from it. I watch his tongue and almost groan, he doesn't play fair.

The Forgotten

"Follow me, Brawler," he orders, and I groan at the nickname before following him across the bunker. He goes around all the big patrol teams, nodding in greeting before we reach the very edge where a strange vehicle sits. All the others are like trucks and RV's. This is...a fucking tank. It's obvious he has spent a long time modding it out and I whistle appreciatively. Metal panels cover nearly every inch of the car, the windows have bars over them, and when he opens the boot he reveals a fucking armoury. I have to bite my lip to hold in my smile, it suits him. A big fucking truck filled with sharp, deadly things. He throws a bag from the floor inside and shuts up the back before turning to me.

"We have been asked to pull an all night patrol, to check out a certain sector that a patrol noted earlier as being occupied. You will follow everything I say or I will tie you inside the car." He arches his eyebrow and I grin.

"Yes, sir," I mock, making him grunt again.

"Get in, Brawler," he throws over his shoulder, as he makes his way to the driver's seat, my eyes locked on his ass.

"We really need to work on my nickname, Beast," I call, drag- ging my eyes away to make my way around the car. I have to grab onto a safety bar inside and yank myself in, it's that tall.

"No, we don't," he says, revving up the car and facing the bunker door as a siren starts to sound, making me jump. The bastard just grins. "Hold on, you are about to see the Wastes."

We share a grin as the large white bunker door starts to roll up, excitement courses through my body, everything I've been working for coming to light, even everything my parents worked for. I just hope it's worth the sacrifice of losing my best friend.

The first thing I notice is it's bright, real fucking bright...and warm, did I mention it's warm? We pull out of the bunker and the heat hits me immediately. I basically have my nose stuck to the glass as I try to take everything in. I hear Jago snigger, but I ignore him. It's so...desolate. Nothing but sand and broken parts of buildings and dead trees surround us as we carve a path through the Waste. With each passing mile, my heart drops and reality comes crashing in. I knew it would be bad out here, but I never expected this! Where is humanity? Where are the people trying to rebuild? Instead, it looks like nature has taken over and the world just gave up.

"Not what you expected?" Jago asks, his voice soft and not filled with condemnation or teasing. Sighing, I sit back and look out of the front window.

"Not really, are we the only ones left?" I inquire, something we are not supposed to question but I need to know.

"Yes and no. The people that are left are...medieval. Fighters, some of the worst of humanity, and children that grew up knowing nothing else. The world is a dark place now, filled with death and people who will kill you for a ration." Looking around us I can imagine that and it makes me feel grateful for the sanctuary of Paradise. I can't imagine going hungry or having to fight continu- ally, not even knowing if you are safe to sleep.

"Well, fuck a duck. I bet I could get a good tan though," I joke, unable to stop myself from breaking the tension. He doesn't roll his eyes like Evan would, he snorts and look over at me.

He carries on driving and I watch our surroundings, trying to keep upbeat. "Want to play a game?" I ask and I hear him grunt. "I am taking that as a yes, a grunting yes sooo... I spy with my little eye something beginning with s." I turn to look at him to see him eyeing me. "This is the part where you guess, I can see how you are confused. I bet no one ever played with little beastie!" I grin as his eyes narrow.

"Don't call me that," he groans when I just keep staring. "Fine, I don't know, fucking sand?" He sounds so put out I can't help but laugh.

"No silly. That would be f," I tease.

"Sand Brawler, you see sand," he says, his voice pained, making me grin.

"Yep! You're turn!" I chirp cheerfully and he stares at me again. "You're weird, do you know that? Why don't you react like a normal person?" He sounds more confused than anything and I just shrug.

"Normal isn't a thing. You have boring people and people who are trying to impress the boring people. I chose to be neither. I don't give a shit what those jerking jackapotmauses think. And it's still your turn."

He groans again even as his lips twitch. "Fine. I spy something beginning with b."

I pretend to think, tapping my chin. "Is it boobs? Because, dude, you really need to stop looking at them. I mean I stare at your ass, but it's rude to point out that you are ogling my assets."

"It's not boobs," he says with a long suffering sigh.

"Wow, so you don't even look at my boobs? Now I'm offended, I mean I know they aren't huge but I think they still are pretty nice, you know? Good handful and nice little nipples." To reinforce my point I pull down my top and grab one.

"Fucking hell, Brawler." The car slams to a stop as he gapes at me, my tit still out between us.

Tilting my head with an innocent expression I blink at him. "Yes?"

He sputters, gesturing at the tit. "You can't just sit there talking about your tits and taking them out! I would have fucking crashed."

I look around pointedly. "Into what? Sand, nothingness? Plus, you brought them up," I explain sullenly and he stares at me incredulously, seemingly lost for words.

"I didn't bring up your tits, you did!" His voice is getting higher and higher.

"Wow, okay, someone is defensive. It's just a boob dude." I shove said boob back in my top.

He stares at me, his mouth hanging open, and I get bored of just sitting here. Leaning forward I flick his nose. "Boop, now was it bricks?" I ask and he shakes his head. Looking back to the road then to me a few times.

"No? Okay, was it bacon? Please say it was bacon, we had it once on a special occasion and I still have wet dreams about it."

"I don't know how to respond to that," he admits, turning and pulling the handbrake as we start back through the Wastes.

Shrugging, I look back out the window. "Was it...oh! Was it Brawler?" I say, turning to see his cheeks heat a little.

"Yes," he mumbles and I grin widely.

"Aww, little beasty. That's so cute," I coo and he grunts, tightening his hands on the steering wheel.

"Fuck off," he grumbles and I grin wider.

"See, I knew you liked me and not just for my boobs."

He groans painfully. "Please, can we stop talking about your boobs?"

"Fiinee, wanna talk about yours?" I respond sweetly.

"Give me fucking strength," I hear him mutter under his breath. "Dude, we aren't in Fallout. You can't pick your character's attributes," I point out helpfully.

"Fallout?" he asks, sounding like he really wishes he hadn't asked.

"Yep, it's a cool game. Evan and I snuck into the media lounge for guards once and they had this old school station and game."

"You and Evan okay now?" he asks, instantly plummeting my mood.

"No," I confess and look out of the window, not wanting to talk about it. I feel him stare at me but I concentrate on the outside world.

"Look, whatever you two are fighting about, you will figure it out," he grunts out as I squint, something catching my eye.

"Uh, Jago?" I question, and he carries on, completely ignoring me.

"Like, I see the way you two are. You will sort it." I nod and poke his arm. He brushes me off and carries on. "Did you two used to be a thing, is that why?" His rambling is cute but I really need him to listen to me.

"I'm touching myself!" I shout and he swerves before righting the car. When he does, he glares over at me.

"What the fuck, Brawler?" he shouts, but his eyes drop to my lap.

"Sorry, needed your attention and it worked, didn't it?"

"I almost crashed, what the fuck is so important?" he says, exasperated.

"Oh, you know. Nothing apart from the gang of bikes speeding towards us," I comment sweetly.

He stares out my window, his eyes widening as he searches around us. He obviously spots what he's searching for before he yanks the wheel to the side, speeding up. "They are too far out, hopefully they won't see us with all the sand kicking up from the bikes," he mutters, talking to himself as I keep an eye on the bikes out the back window.

He swerves again and again until I lose track, my eyes locked on the last spot I saw the bikes.

"Still see them?" he asks, and I look back to see his face tight and his hands clenched on the wheel.

"No, we lost them," I say and he nods.

"Good, we need to lay low and let them pass," he instructs as he races through what looks like it used to be a town.

Broken buildings, including a church with overgrown nature surrounding them, line the once road, which is now covered in holes. I don't get long to look around before he pulls into what looks like it used to be a building of some sort, a tight one room attached to an old crumbling cottage. He gets out the car and I slip out, having to squeeze since the walls are that close. He throws out the bags and weapons onto the road, and grabs a tarp from inside. He throws one side to me and I catch it, working wordlessly and feeling his growing panic. I wonder if he is panicking because I am here and he feels the need to protect me. He yanks the tarp over the top and I follow until it's tucked all around the car. Hiding it.

He steps back with a frown, and I realise what he's trying to do. Wanting to help, I scurry outside and grab armfuls of broken debris, signs, wood, and sand. He glares when I come back in and fling it haphazardly on the car. His smile starts small but breaks into a full grin when he sees where I am going. We work silently and quickly. Covering the car until it blends in with the building. Stepping back, I nod and he grabs a bag, while I grab the others and turn to the cottage, guessing that is where we are staying.

"Nope. We don't want to be caught too close to the car if they find it," he grunts and I nod, following him across the road. His head is constantly swivelling, his eyes searching for threats. He looks like he belongs out here and as dangerous as it is, he seems more. Like he is more confident out here in the Wastes and the forgotten than he ever was in Paradise, and I must admit my heart thumps with the excitement and danger.

We make it across the road and around the back of what looks like an old shop when I hear the rumbling of bikes. I flatten my back against the wall and Jago positions himself in front of me, dropping the bag on the floor and grabbing two knives. I eye them and him.

"Don't I get a weapon?" I whisper and he grunts. Rolling his eyes he reaches down and passes me a thin looking sword. It's small, tinier than the others, and I eye it. It fits in my hand perfectly and is curved up at the end.

"What is it?" I whisper and he looks down at me.

"A katana, I thought it would be easier for you to use. Smaller grip but still deadly, takes some training to be able to use properly though." I grin as he keeps his eyes searching around us. He thought about me when grabbing weapons, so much so that he picked out a weapon for me. For a man like Jago, that is practically a gift, and it might be smaller but size isn't everything...

He turns to face me as the rumbling gets louder, shaking the broken building against my back. I should be scared, but I can't seem to stop the excitement and adrenaline pumping through my blood. He stares down at me, a grin dancing on his face and that same excitement is there in his eyes. He might not admit it, but he likes the fight. He likes the excitement and danger out here. He puts his hand to his lips in a shush gesture, the knife glinting against the soft flesh of his mouth. I nod and lean back, he shuffles closer, not leaving an inch between our bodies.

Licking my lips, I try to drag my eyes away from his mouth, but all that excitement is morphing to lust with nothing to fight. He must be feeling the same because he lets out a silent groan, his body shaking against mine, and I meet his eyes I see the lust dancing there. Those fiery eyes are burning me up and making me pant as his hips push against mine, pinning me there.

I open my mouth, but I don't know what to say when the rumbling stops right behind us. They obviously stopped their bikes in the middle of the road. I hear them talking, even as Jago smashes his lips to mine obviously trying to keep me quiet, but when I tangle my tongue with his he pushes closer, grabbing my face, the cool steel of the knife against my overheated cheek as he devours me.

I reach up, placing my hands around his neck, as the katana hangs down his back. His hips push against me and I groan into his mouth. He pulls back and nips my lip as punishment. I keep an ear out for the people on the bikes, but I can hear them chattering amongst themselves as they search the buildings.

To my disappointment, he pulls away and buries his face in my neck, breathing heavily. "You are distracting me," he mutters and I grin.

I lean into him, whispering against his skin so we don't draw any attention. "Keep your eyes and ears out for them," I warn, licking along his sweaty skin. He shivers against me.

"What?" he questions, his voice thick with lust.

"Keep watch," I reply, snaking my hand down his rock-hard stomach until I flick open the button of his jeans. He freezes but doesn't stop me. He loves this as much as I do, the thought of being caught, the danger lurking around the corner.

I bury my hand in his pants, curling around his already hard cock, and grinning when I feel the pre-cum at the tip.

"Brawler," he growls in warning, and I squeeze his cock in reply, he thrusts into my hand. I lick along his neck again as he pants into my skin.

Pumping up and down I work him hard and fast. He fucks himself into my hand, grunting into my neck. Needing better access, I reach down with my other hand, trusting him to watch my back as I push down his jeans. He helps me, wiggling out of them until they rest around his ankles. Stilling pumping his length I reach down and cup his balls, squeezing his cock at the same time as we hear a man's voice drawing closer. He thrusts hard, his body shaking as he bites into my neck to stifle his roar as he comes.

We both freeze as the voice moves closer, all the man needs to do is round the corner and he will find us. Pulling back, Jago swears, his mind instantly back on business. He reaches down and pulls up his jeans, but he doesn't get time to button them before we hear the voice, closer than ever before. He flattens his back against the wall in front of me, his hands holding both knives as he waits like a cobra, his cock still hanging from his pants.

We wait for what seems like forever. Sweat drips down my face and in between my breasts, and I dare not even breathe. Eventually we hear the footsteps moving away and Jago lets out a breath. Looking at me he raises his eyebrow. Determined to wipe that worried look off his face, I bring my hand covered in his cum to my mouth and lick. His eyes widen and lust bursts to life in his eyes as he watches me clean my hand. I spot his cock hardening out of the corner of my eye and he doesn't look away from me.

"Yum," I whisper, bending down and grabbing my sword once again as we hear the bikes restart as they pull away, leaving the town, obviously getting what they were searching for.

"You are going to pay for that," he warns, spinning towards me. "Can't wait," I tease, as he slams me into the wall and smashes his lips back to mine. I groan and hold on as he fucks my mouth with his tongue. He pulls away as fast as it started. "We need to get inside, wait them out until we are sure they aren't coming back."

I nod in a daze and he grins, he grabs our stuff and I follow him back around the building. Fuck, if this is what patrol is like then sign me up every fucking day.

Chapter 9
Love Nest

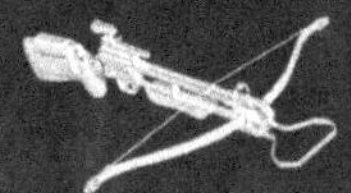

We don't venture too far from the car, just into an abandoned building opposite. We take the second floor of what looks like abandoned flats, as the first floor has a massive hole in the front of the building. The stairs are rickety, have holes, and are covered in debris, but Jago points out we will hear someone coming.

When we reach the second floor I cover my nose at the smell, it stinks of decay and rot, and it's almost pitch-black up here apart from the light streaming through the window. Walking down the dusty hallway, Jago picks a door at the end. The bloody wood with a wonky 2A on the front. He twists the handle and it opens without needing a key or to be kicked in. When he swings it open we both wait and I almost scream as a rat scurries out. Jago grins over at me and walks inside, flicking the light switch. Not surprisingly it doesn't work. I keep the door open to let the light in and squint, but I can't see anything. Jago makes his way around the room and I lose sight of him. Shifting on my feet I start to get nervous without him by my side. I keep looking over my shoulder until I hear a bang from inside the flat.

"Jago?" I whisper and I hear a grunt before light streams in, making my eyes water from straining hard in the dark. He coughs as he throws the dirty curtain to the floor.

Looking around, sadness blooms in my chest. This was someone's home. Pictures of two men with a small child adorn the walls and the mantel above the fireplace. It was perfectly decorated before the world ended, now it's run down and left behind. The pictures are cracked and dusty, with some falling to the floor. The coffee table is overturned and the sofa is covered in a layer of dust and mould. The room is a long rectangle with a living room to the left and a divider to the right, with a counter where you can see into a kitchen. Walking in, I shut the door softly behind me and explore the kitchen. Running my hand across the marble countertop I leave a clean smear in my wake. The stainless steel fridge stands closed and I know better than to open that with the power being out for so long. Cupboards run under the worktop and above it, screwed to the ceil- ing. The once white doors are dirty and decayed, and some are hanging from their hinges. It's obvious this place has been ransacked. Poking my head around the corridor leading to the rest of the flat, I hesitate before forcing myself down it. More pictures line the walls with three doors leading off at the end. The first is a bathroom, and apart from being a bit dirty and the stale air, it's not bad. The second is a child's room and I quickly shut that, not wanting to see it. The last is a master bedroom. A huge king-sized bed sits in the middle of the room with the bedding perfectly made. This room looks untouched but a waft of stale air hits me when I open the door. I shut it quietly and go back to the living room to see Jago unpacking.

He grabs a blanket and lays it on the floor, and grabs two canteens next. He also adds some rations and a few weapons before pushing the sofa up against the front door. I watch him the whole time, but he doesn't even seem to realise I am here. It is apparent he has done this a lot, his natural routine and confidence telling me all I need to know. Next he positions a chair under the window with what looks like a sniper rifle.

Once done he looks around and spots me in the hallway, and he watches me, obviously wondering why I am just staring at him.

"You are like one of those old-style housewives, all you need is an apron," I tease, and he shakes his head and I grin. Sometimes I think he has got the hang of the whole talking thing, and then some- times he retreats to being a wild animal.

Still smiling, I plop myself down on the blanket and stare at the mouldy ceiling. "Who were they?" I ask as I hear him settle into the chair by the window, keeping watch.

"From one of the clans," he says, and I lift my head to see him staring out the window.

"Clans?" I ask, confused.

"There are four that I know of, spread around the Wastes. They band together for safety and survival. The Worshippers, some crazy bastards, are closer to us than I like. The Seekers, pray you never run into them. Reeves, they tend to be dumb but good fighters, probably who was out there."

"The last?" I press, rolling to my side to see him.

"Berserkers, I only ran into them once and it was enough to leave an impression. Cruel fucking warriors."

If they are enough to freak out even Jago then I need to stay clear from them. "Do they know about us?" I ask, trying to work through all this new information. If Jago knows, surely the leaders of Paradise do as well. So why didn't they tell us?

He hesitates, and for the first time since I met him, lies to me. "No," he grunts but I see his eye twitch.

"You are a shitty liar. If you can't tell me the truth then don't tell me at all. At least give me that decency." I roll back to face the ceiling when I hear him sigh.

"It's to protect you," he admits and I feel his eyes on me.

"That's okay, but don't lie. I am not a child that needs that." I start to get angry, chafing at the treatment. I thought he saw me as an equal, maybe I was wrong.

"Brawler," he says softly and I ignore him to stare at the ceiling.

I hear him moving before he appears above me, making me yelp. "Damn it, you need a fucking bell or something!" I shout, slapping his solid chest as he lays on top of me. "I'm serious, I'm going to make you a collar with one if you want to act like a..." I sputter and he grins, those eyes sparkling.

"Beast?" he finishes, winking at me, and making me smile. I sigh and lean my head back. "Why don't I show you how much of a beast I am?" His voice is low and rumbly, making things clench low in my body.

"Shouldn't you be on watch?" I ask, but my hands are already wandering up his chest to wrap around his neck.

"I will hear them coming," he says cockily. "Just like I plan on hearing you coming."

I groan at the pun. "Leave the jokes to me. Well then, better put your mouth where your thigh is." I grin when he laughs, pushing his thigh harder into my pussy. Spreading my legs I let him have access, needing him as much as he needs me. We were interrupted the other day and it's all I keep thinking about. Every touch, every flirty word or look has been driving me to a fever point, until all I want is his cock buried in me, fucking me like the beast he is.

He doesn't waste any more time or words, he leans his head down and locks our lips together. Teasing me with little bites and soft kisses before I open and he slips his tongue inside, dominating my mouth as we tangle for control.

Holding himself above me with one hand, he uses the other to pull my top down, baring my breasts to the air. I groan as he covers one with his big hand, tweaking my nipple. He pulls away from my mouth to whisper against me. "I nearly threw you over my knee and fucked you in the car when you showed me these earlier," he admits, nudging my face to the side and kissing down my neck.

His lips wrap around one nipple and I arch into his mouth, he moves to the other and lavishes the same treatment before licking down my stomach. "Didn't I say I'd make you pay?" he whispers against my skin, making goosebumps raise in his wake.

"Nope, definitely not. I think what you said was, 'oh Piper, you are a goddess who I will bestow lots and lots of orgasms on.'"

He lifts his head, his eyebrow arched as he watches me.

"Totally did, now get to it. Orgasm please," I order, and he grins before leaning down and licking me. Dropping my head back to the blanket I grip it at my sides as he goes to town on my pussy. Licking around my nub before dipping inside my tight channel. Moans slip from my lips but he doesn't speed up, just keeps me on edge.

"Fucking prick," I gasp as he sucks on my nub.

He moves over me again, his face hard and brutal. Fuck, why does it turn me on so much when he is like this?

"Punishment, Brawler," he whispers. I gulp at the intensity in his eyes.

He grabs both of my legs, spreading them before pushing my knees back to my chest. "Hold them there, and don't fucking move," he orders.

He drops his head back to my pussy and slips two fingers into me, stretching me as his tongue circles my clit. He pulls them out of me fast, curling them on his stroke back in. I moan, my legs shaking and dropping gently and he nips at my thigh in punishment. Grip- ping my knees so tightly my fingers whiten. I writhe, trying to push closer to his mouth as the orgasm starts to build. He sucks my clit into his mouth and I scream, but he withdraws his fingers and I am left pant- ing, on the verge of coming.

"Jago," I moan.

"Punishment, Brawler," he repeats.

Opening my eyes I glare at him, his beard is wet with my juices and he looks mighty fucking proud of himself.

"Fine," I grumble, dropping my knees and flicking my clit with my own fingers. Running my other hand to my chest I tweak my nipple, my eyes on him as he watches me hungrily.

Running my fingers down my wet pussy, I watch him bite his lip before he leans forward and grabs my thighs, pushing them wide open so he can see. Slipping two fingers inside myself I moan as I arch into my own touch.

"Let me see you come," he demands.

"Happy to oblige," I say, breathless as I tweak my nipple and groan as I come, my channel tightening on my fingers as my legs shake. Pulling my fingers out, I gasp when he drops himself between my legs and rams inside of me.

He pulls out before slamming back in, gripping my thighs and throwing them over his shoulders before grabbing my arse and dragging me closer. Pushing back, I grip the blanket as I meet him thrust for thrust, our eyes locked on each other before he bends down and kisses me hard. Dropping my legs to around his waist I kick his arse, pushing him harder, faster.

"Fuck, you're so tight," he groans into my mouth.

He pulls out suddenly and flips me, my face in the blanket as he grips my hips meanly and drags me into the air. With no warning he thrusts back in, stretching me. Panting hard, I push back, meeting his thrusts as his hand skates up my back to wrap around my hair.

Twisting it, he pulls my head to the side as he fucks me hard and fast. My neck twinges but I ignore it all as he fucks me like he owns me. Kissing me again, he swallows the moans leaving my lips.

Ripping away from him I suck in a breath and he bites down my neck to my ear. "Come for me, let me feel your wet pussy clamp around my cock," he demands.

His words throw me over again and he follows me, yelling his release before clamping his teeth onto my shoulder to mute the sound.

We both collapse onto the sofa, his weight heavy but comforting as we try to relearn how to breathe.

Sitting in just my panties and bra, I use my fingers to get the food from the tin, watching Jago as he alternates between eating and looking out of the window in his unbuttoned jeans. Even now, with the ache between my thighs and his bite marks along my neck, I want him again.

He's barefoot, and for some reason that is driving me crazy. He sticks his finger in the tin before licking it clean, making me bite my lip to stop from groaning. Shuffling on the mat to try and relieve the pressure, I watch him eat even as he's oblivious to my stare.

When he finishes and puts the tin down to the side, and his gaze is locked through the window and somewhere in the distance. I raise from our little nest and saunter to him. I drop myself in his lap and he catches me automatically, his head turning as his lips curls up.

His mouth opens but I put my finger to his lips. "I need you," I admit, and I see the lust flare again in his eyes as his hands clench on my waist. He is frozen as I wiggle free and drop to my knees in front of him.

"This way you can keep watch." I grin as his eyes flare and his tongue darts out to wet his lips.

I tug on his jeans and he raises his ass to help me pull them over his thick thighs to tangle at his feet, restricting his movements.

His cock springs free, already hard and ready for me, making me lick my lips and he groans, his hand reaching out and tangling in my hair as he tugs me wordlessly to his waiting cock. He might not be great with words, but he always finds a way to show me what he wants. Blowing a breath over the head of his cock, his fingers tighten in my hair in warning. Grinning, I lick the slit before licking around his rim, my eyes locking on his. They burn brighter than the sun as he stares at me like I am enchanting him.

He growls and yanks my head again, and letting him control me, I open my mouth as he thrusts his cock into it. Groaning at the taste of him I sink further down until I can't reach the bottom, and I have to wrap my other hand around the base. He doesn't wait for me to get comfortable or offer any warning before dragging my head back up and pushing me back down. I love being independent and strong, but there is something about this tough warrior controlling and dominating me that has me wet and needy. He gives me no choice but to give up control to him, to let him be in control of everything. It pushes all my worries and usually wandering mind to the side until all I can think about is him.

Hollowing my cheeks, I start to hum as he works me up and down his length. His fingers tighten painfully in my hair as I rub myself on the floor. A rough, primal groan comes from his throat, driving me wild.

He thrusts up, using his feet against the floor, before growling and ripping me away from his pulsing cock. I moan in need as he reaches down and yanks me onto his lap. He doesn't even bother taking off the bra I am wearing, just reaches between our bodies and flicks my clit, before burying his fingers in my waiting pussy.

"Fuck, you are so wet," he groans, rubbing me inside before pulling out and thrusting back in. Wiggling on his lap I gasp, grabbing his shoulders I hold on and ride his hand. The orgasm sneaks up on me and I have to bite my lips so I don't scream. The shock waves are still riding me as he pulls his fingers out, and lines his cock up with my entrance, thrusting up into me.

We both moan as I dig my nails into his shoulders, shaking from the force. He doesn't give me time to adjust, just starts fucking me hard until I am bouncing on his cock, holding on to him.

"Ride me, Brawler," he growls and I moan, I fucking love his dirty mouth. Doing as I am told for once, I use my grip to fuck myself on him, rising up and bouncing back down. He groans, the sound doing things to me, and I lean down and cover his lips, needing to taste him even with the aftertaste of his pre-cum in my mouth.

His hands grip my arse, hard enough to bruise as he helps me, up and down, up and down as we devour each other's mouths. Fighting for control, holding onto each other like the light in the dark. The world outside is dead, I can hear the growls of something feral out there before a howl splits the air and still I moan into his mouth, riding him, knowing he will keep me safe when I can't protect myself. Jago, Beast, my protector.

The Forgotten

"Fuck, come for me. Let me feel you milking my cock and coming apart in my arms." His voice is breathless and hard, and I scream into his mouth as he thrusts up, harder than before, and bumps my cervix. It throws me over the edge and he follows after me, both of us swallowing each other's yell of pleasure until we are shaking and wrung dry, holding onto each other as we relearn how to breathe.

My eyes open slowly as his fingers stroke my cheek, his eyes are soft and staring at me with wonder, so of course I have to say something to spoil the mood. "Do you have any wet wipes?" I blurt out and he snorts.

Chapter 10
Cumbuckets

It is just starting to get dark when Jago grunts and starts packing away.

"We leaving?" I ask, sprawled on the floor, finally fully dressed again.

"Yup, haven't heard bikes in two hours or seen any, we need to patrol our sector and report back," he says, still packing his gun and other bits and bobs away.

Nodding, I jump up to help, and within five minutes we have everything packed away again. When we go to leave, I look back at the flat, hoping whoever lived here managed to survive even though I am betting they didn't. Closing the door, I see Jago waiting for me at the stairs. His face is blank but when I smile at him, he returns it and my breath catches. I love Evan, more than anything in the world. It was a love that grew from secrets and shared pain, but this? This is wild and untam- able, roaring through me with the power to destroy me. It doesn't mean I don't love Evan less, just differently. It's weak, but it's there, and I know looking into Jago's eyes that I could love him.

"Ready?" he inquires, completely oblivious to my inner turmoil. I nod mutely and follow after him down the stairs, he grabs my hand and pulls me around the safe bits, testing every step like he doesn't trust it. He only let's go when we are at the bottom so he can open the front door. My palm still tingles from the contact, but I force my mind back to business, patrol.

He peeks out around the door, scanning our surroundings, before stepping out. Only when he reaches back and pulls me forward do I follow, trusting his instincts and knowledge. Without being told, I skim around the building with him, sticking to the shadows in the dying light just in case anyone is there.

We cross the road quickly, keeping low and not prolonging the exposure in such open air, and when we get back to the car we find it undisturbed. Without him having to prompt me, I start clearing it and we load back up quickly.

I make sure to keep a clear watch now that I know how easy it is to be snuck up on, my scanning the horizon is only interrupted by sharing smiles with Jago. He is downright cheerful for the usually angry beast, his eyes dancing with happiness even as he flicks them across everything, searching. At one point, he even takes his hand off the wheel and squeezes my thigh before gripping it again.

I have to bite my lip to hold in my smile, feeling all warm and happy inside. I know it was just sex, but over the course of my training with him, something was growing, something more than just desire. I mean sure, that was there too, I am not a blind old lady with a dry fanny, but the trust and confidence he has in me...

Shaking my head, not willing to get distracted I keep my eye out of the window. "I spy something beginning with...H," I say and I hear him grunt out a laugh.

"House?" he asks, driving through another burnt down suburb and back into the Wastes.

"Nope," I respond cheerfully.

"Hell?" he guesses and I turn with my mouth open.

"Was that a joke, did you make a joke? Damn, I really am rubbing off on you! Next, you will be drinking coffee," I tease and he shakes his head.

"You shouldn't drink that shit," he murmurs, still looking around as he flicks on the headlights, lighting up the dirt road.

"Okay, new game. Question game," I say, leaning my head back as I look out the window.

"Question game?" he asks.

"Yup, we each get to ask a question. If you don't answer you have to forfeit," I reply cheerfully and he grunts. "I am taking that as I yes, I will even start. How old were you when you came to Paradise?" I question, curious.

He blows out a breath and when I look over, it looks like he is fighting with himself on whether or not to answer me.

"Seriously, dude. You know I will just keep bugging you or get my tits out again."

That makes him smile. "Thirteen." One word, but I hear the pain in it.

"So, had your balls dropped by then?" I ask, the words slipping out.

He chokes and I laugh as he glares over at me, looking exasperated. "My turn." I nod and he thinks as I stare back out the window again. "Were you and that doc dating?"

Interesting that is his first question, and I hide my grin, knowing he won't appreciate it, by staring into the dark. Mulling over what to say, I reply with, "Nope, I thought at one point we would, but we are...friends."

"You love him?" he presses.

Three simple words, an innocent question, but holding a wealth of meaning. "Uh uh, that's not how the game works Beast. My turn, why did you come to Paradise?"

"Brawler," he warns. "What's the forfeit?"

"To be decided by the other person," I answer and he sighs. "Forfeit," he grumbles, and it hurts that he won't trust me with it but I understand as well.

"Your turn," I say, looking over at him with a smile so he knows there are no hard feelings.

"Why do you want to patrol?" he inquires slowly. "I already told you that," I tease.

"Is it because of your parents? You won't find them alive out here and living happily ever after, and there isn't a life out here to escape to," he finishes and I stiffen in my seat.

"I know that," I snark, getting defensive.

He looks over at me and I stare into his eyes, showing him the truth. He nods and I look back out of the window.

"Favorite position?" I ask and I hear him snort again, making me grin into the night, the headlights lighting our way.

The rest of patrol is boring, we play the question game for a while before Jago starts to tell me about some of the other patrols and gives me more insight into the workings. I lap it up, knowing I will need as much help as possible. When the light of day starts to burn through the sky my heart drops, because I know it means we have to go back. It might be dead and scary out here, but the freedom, the air, it's like nothing I can describe and I know I am not meant to live down there in that bunker. I feel it in my soul, one day I will leave. I wonder if they will come with me...

Shaking my head free of the silly thoughts, I yawn when we pull up to the electrified chain-link gate. Jago gets out and points at the camera before getting back in, it opens automatically and we roll through, and around the building that stands proxy and to the back where the huge bunker door stands hidden. We ride down the ramp, a few other patrol vehicles in front of us, waiting for it to open.

"Does it stay locked all night?" I ask, curious even as my body wants me to sleep. Exhaustion pulling at me.

"Yes, it only opens at two times. Once in the evening for night patrol to change with day, and once in the morning."

I nod, makes sense.

"Still want to be patrol, Brawler?" he questions, looking at me, and I manage to grin.

"Fuck yes."

He grunts with a smile and pulls forward into the hangar as the door rolls up. I jump out and start unpacking with him, both of us sharing flirty little touches between us and shared smiles until a man walks over. I've never seen him before, but when Jago spots him his face loses all emotion and he stiffens. It makes me do a double take of the man. He's around my height with more muscle than skin, but he has a scary fucking face. His grey hair is pulled tight to his head, and his clothes are pressed within an inch of its life. He walks like he has a stick up his arse.

"Anything?" he barks, not even addressing Jago. He looks over us and stops on me, his eyebrow raises as he pursues me, it feels vaguely sexual, but when he meets my eyes again all I see is disgust. "Ah yes, I heard about the little girl playing patrol," he mocks, his voice filled with contempt. I wonder if he would look like that if I ripped his dick off and whacked him on the face with it.

Instead of letting my mouth run wild, I smile sweetly at him, opening my mouth to respond, but Jago steps in front of me, a hand coming up and covering my mouth like he knows I was going to say something stupid. "Just a few bikes to the north, nothing close and not recurring," he grunts, his voice thick with hate for the man.

The man huffs and starts to walk away before looking back. "She's your responsibility, if she fails, so do you," he warns before walking away.

I can feel the steel running through Jago's back so I dart my tongue out and lick his palm, and he looks down at me, eyeing me strangely.

I start to mumble against his palm and he drops his hand. "Don't get me wrong, I will try anything once, but I don't think I am into being gagged." I wink and he groans, smirking down at me.

"Come on, let's get out of here." He shuts the door before slinging both packs over his arms.

"Was that a weird sexual offer, cause I reckon I am too tired, but you could just put the tip in if you want...or wait until I am asleep, it doesn't really matter to me..." I carry on and follow after him as he tries to escape me, looking downright pained with the conversation.

"Brawler," he whines and I smile.

"Fine, I will try to stay awake," I concede and he turns to me, staring at me like he doesn't know what to say, most people don't. "Least let me wash up first, there is sand in places there shouldn't be," I warn.

"Lovely image, thank you," he snorts.

"You're welcome, just something to think about!" I pat his shoulder and skip away merrily, even though I am tired, I have never felt so alive.

I hum on my way back to my place and quickly strip off, the clothes feeling horrible after the sex and sand. Fuck, my vagina sweated out there, not cool.

I jump in the shower and scrub at my skin and hair, I let the water wash away the sand, but I am nearly asleep standing up so I grab a towel and wrap it around me, letting my hair drip down as I walk back into my room. I freeze once there, seeing Evan hesitating inside the door as if he isn't sure if he should be here.

"Evvi-Evan?" I ask, stumbling so as not to use his nickname. His shoulders slump and he looks over at me, unable to hide the worry and heartache in his eyes.

"I just... wanted to make sure you were okay," he says softly, his eyes darting down my body before he looks away.

When he doesn't look back I clench my jaw. "Fine." He nods and turns around to leave. "Good."

Then he walks out and I just stand there, dripping on the tiles as I watch the door close after him. Letting my head fall back I groan at the ceiling. Men, they can be such cumbuckets.

Chapter 11
Work Me Hard

I crashed hard last night, not even bothering to get dressed before I crawled under the covers and fell deeply asleep, so when banging sounds at a god awful time in the morning, I groan and bury myself in the covers, ignoring it. It comes again and I growl. "Go away, I am having an orgy!" I shout, before curling back under the covers. I must nod back off, because when I hear the door slide open I yelp and scramble to get up, only to fall off my bed and land on my naked ass on the cold tiles.

Peering sadly up at Jago, it soon turns into a glare. He laughs, leaning against the wall as he watches me. "What the hell dude?" I ask, jumping up and placing my hands on my hips.

He sobers up as his eyes drop to my body, and I grin. "Eyes up here buddy!" I point and he rolls his.

"Time for training," he announces, staring at my tits again. "Crazy person say what?" I whine.

"Yup. It seems you have caught the captain's attention. He is determined not to have a woman on patrol, so if you are serious about it, we need to prove him wrong. You will train from four AM until dinner, get some rest, and then you will patrol with me all night."

"Huh?" I question, slow on the uptake from the lack of sleep and caffeine—did I mention caffeine?

"Get dressed." He points at me.

"Why are you helping me?" I ask, crossing my arms under my breasts and he groans, trying to look away.

"Because if you fail, I fail. I don't fail ever, so get your cute ass dressed so I can work you to death." He sounds pained.

"You think I'm cute? Also, I am really hoping you were talking about sex because if you woke me up to fight or run, I am going to be pissed," I warn.

"What about if I tell you I snuck you two coffees?" He brings them from around his back and I zero in on them. Running forward I snatch them both and hold them to my chest, looking up at him with a dreamy smile.

"Okay, I take that back, but after these, I am still down for a bit of *training*." I wink and he shakes his head.

"Real training," he warns and I groan.

"Where's the fun in that? No orgasm? You are mean." I wander away, sipping at the coffee before grabbing some clothes.

"Just...just get dressed."

When I look over my shoulder, his eyes are locked on my ass, and he looks like he is about two seconds away from throwing me on the bed, hell yeah.

I decide to take pity on him, he is the bringer of coffee so I have to be nice. I get dressed and down both before looking back at him. "Okay, Beast. Let's go."

"I hate you, I am never sucking your dick again. You will have to learn to do it by yourself," I lament, flopping back onto the mat in a sweaty mess, and guess what? No orgasms. Just pure torture.

He laughs and sits down next to me, reaching out to massage my legs even as I glare at him. "I mean it, I was even going to let you do me in the ass, but now? That train has long gone buster, the only hole you are sticking little beastie in is your fists."

He chokes before he laughs, it roars from him. It's a nice sound and I find my lips twitching, even as I pant and groan. My whole body aches and I am sweating from places you shouldn't sweat from, and what is that fucking smell? Lifting my head I sniff under my arms and grimace. Shower then nap, that's the plan.

He slaps my leg and gets up, his chuckles dying off. "Come on Brawler, you need to stretch out your muscles or you will get stiff." I accept his hand and he pulls me up, holding me to his chest more than he needs to. "You are doing really good," he praises, looking down at me.

"Was that...a compliment?" I act shocked and he grunts. Laughing now, I turn to whip my head around when he spanks me.

"Get washed, you stink," he teases and I narrow my eyes at him. "Oh and you smell like fucking daisies? I don't think so buddy,

might want to wash yourself."

I grin when he glances down, and he thinks I don't notice when he discreetly sniffs himself. Still moaning about my muscles we leave the gym together.

"Want to wash my back?" I wink and wiggle my eyebrows and he glances over, looking confused.

We wait for some guards to pass us before he opens his mouth. "Why, can't you reach it?" His face is scrunched up adorably and I have to bite my lip to hold in my laugh, something tells me he wouldn't appreciate it.

"Sex, I was asking if you wanted to have shower sex," I point out helpfully, and his eyes widen and his mouth opens in an 'O.'

I grin and turn. "Race ya!" I shout and start jogging as I hear him swear and scramble to chase me.

I manage to avoid his grasp until I tumble into my room, he slides in as the door is shutting, and grabs me under my bum and lifts, his mouth sealing on mine. I groan and wrap my legs around him as he walks us backwards.

He fumbles with the shower, holding me with one hand as I tangle my tongue with his. I hear the shower spray come on and I drag my mouth away, panting as I tug on his shirt. He drops me to the floor and yanks it over his head, revealing his washboard abs and adonis belt. I quickly strip as he pulls off his pants, hopping from foot to foot. Grinning, I dart under the spray, slicking my hair back as he jumps in and pushes me into the wall until my breath whooshes from me. I manage to slip away, wagging my finger as I quickly wash my body. He rolls his eyes but copies me, before backing me into the wall again.

He is on me in an instant, kissing me hard before he pulls away, trailing stinging kisses down my neck and then he drops to his knees, pushing my legs apart as his lips wrap around a nipple. Groaning, I lean my head back and grip onto his hair, wrapping it around my fist. He switches to the other one as his hand skates up my thigh, wrapping around it and hoisting it onto his shoulder. Kissing down my stomach, he slides his eyes up as he blows a warm breath on my already wet pussy. I meet his gaze and he licks me, making me wiggle and moan.

Without warning, a finger pushes into me, making me throw my head back and clench my eyes shut. He adds another, stretching me as he teases around my clit with his tongue. His hand wraps around my other thigh, digging in hard enough to bruise and he throws my second leg over his other shoulder and pulls my pussy closer to his mouth. Bracing my back against the wall, I have to trust him to hold me, good job he is strong enough.

"Fuck," I pant, writhing against his mouth as he fucks me with his tongue.

He groans into me, making me push harder against his mouth. His fingers sink into me as he starts to fuck me, curling his tongue around my clit at the same time his fingers find that spot inside of me.

I come apart with a scream and as I am recovering, he drops me to shaky legs, spins me, and pushes my face onto the cool wall. Turning to the side, I pant and shake with aftershocks as he kicks open my legs, making me groan. Why is that so hot?

"Jago," I moan and that only seems to spur him on.

Grunting, he grabs my hands and places them on the wall on either side of me. "They stay there." His voice is rough and hard and I shake at the intensity.

I do as I am told, and his hand runs down my body, goosebumps rising in his wake until he circles my wet pussy again. His hand leaves me and I feel the head of his cock pushing in, stretching me.

He slowly pushes until his balls are pressed against me and then he waits, holding me there until I adjust to his size. Groaning, I push back and he grunts again.

His hand circles my body and grabs my throat, gripping it hard enough to say he means business. My eyes nearly roll back in my head as I push back again, needing him to move.

"Brawler," he warns and squeezes my throat harder. Licking my lips, I grin and do it again. He stills my movement by gripping my hip, his fingers digging in. It will leave a bruise and I love that. His hand leaves my hip once I stop, and he tilts my head around until he can seal his lips over mine, the kiss hard and dominant before he pulls away.

"Be fucking good or you don't come again," he cautions, his fingers digging back into my hip as he starts to move. Shallow thrusts that are more torture than pleasure, but I know he means what he said so I stay there like a good girl and let him fuck himself in and out of me. I can't help the needy little breathless noises leaving me, and every time he hears one, he grunts and thrusts harder, pushing me into the wall.

"Jago, please," I beg.

He growls, both hands tightening as he pulls out and slams back in, fucking me. He does it again and again, slamming me into the wall with his thrusts. His hand on my throat and hips keep me anchored as he fucks me hard and fast, not taking any prisoners until the pain and pleasure mingle together, and I scream my release. He roars and follows me, his cum splashing inside of me as he thrusts once more before stilling.

He stumbles into me and I flatten into the wall, panting and ready to collapse.

"Fuck," he says and I nod, lost for words for once.

Curled up on Jago's chest, I let his breathing lull me to sleep, knowing I need to rest before our night patrol. I figured once we had recovered from our shower scene he would leave and tell me to meet him tonight, but he surprised me. He stayed. He helped me wash my hair and we dried off and fell into bed, both exhausted.

He played with my hair and when I wake up, his hand is still wrapped in it. Tilting my head back I grin when I spot his slack face, peaceful in his sleep. I never really noticed the tightness around his eyes and mouth until now. My hand reaches up before I even realise it, and I am just about to touch his face when his hand darts out and grabs mine. His fiery eyes slowly open and he seems confused, when he looks from my hand hovering over his face to me, he lets go quickly mumbling an apology. I drop my hand back to his face, letting him know I don't care, it's not like he really hurt me. He watches me carefully as I stroke his features, like he is waiting for me to hit him or hurt him in some way. He watches me intently as I map out his face with my fingers. When I get to his lips, he parts them slightly as I run my finger across.

"Piper," he breathes, one of the only times he hasn't called me some form of a nickname.

It makes me swallow hard and glance up, I see the vulnerability in his eyes and I can't help but lean in and drop a soft kiss on those lips. He lies there and lets me, as I peck him again and again before pulling my lips away to look into his eyes. He looks dazed and scared.

Leaning down slowly I kiss him again, he opens his mouth and I sweep in, keeping it soft and sweet. His arms wrap around me as he explores my mouth leisurely. There's no rush, I want him as much as I always do, but I want to show him that this is more than physical, even if he doesn't want to admit it and neither do I. I have been hurt so much, and so recently, that this is crazy, and opening my heart back up is stupid, but I can't help letting him in.

The hours spent training together, the smiles, the jokes, the patrols, all of it piles up until I am telling him with my kiss everything that I can't say. He returns it and I slowly pull away, breathing each other in before I lay my head back on his chest.

He drops a kiss on my head and plays with my hair again as he holds me to him, smiling I look at the clock and groan.

"What is it, Brawler?" he asks, his voice rough.

"We need to get up," I say, even as I reach out and start drawing patterns on his chest.

He sighs, obviously not wanting to move as much as I do, so I lean up and drop a kiss on his lips before sliding out of bed. He watches me as I nip to the bathroom, and when I get back I see he is still in bed, his arm behind his head as he smiles at me.

I roll my eyes and grab some clothes and get dressed. I hear him sigh and his feet hit the floor as he gets up and clothed. When I have laced my shoes, I glance up to see he's already finished. Damn, how the fuck did he do that?

I walk towards him and grin and leaning up, I drop a kiss on his lips, knowing out there we will have to pretend again. He grins against my lips as I pull away, his hand lingering on mine as I turn.

Like he can't help himself, he reaches out and pulls me back, spinning until I fall into his chest. Without missing a beat he tilts my chin up and kisses me, it's hard and hot and I moan as he pulls away, a smile in place to show me he knows exactly what he is doing.

"Come on, Brawler. Time to patrol." He spanks me and I glare at him.

We pack up for patrol quickly, already late, and wait for the bunker door to open. I ignore all the other teams and the looks we are getting. Looking down at the map Jago gave me, I quickly map out the route he showed me while we wait.

I hear the siren and the door rolls open, we line up with the others and make our way out of Paradise, passing the day patrol coming in.

Once we hit that stretch of road, the others break off and it feels like I can breathe easier again.

"I have a new game," I say with a grin and he groans, making me laugh.

Looking over at him we share a smile and I start to explain, he throws me looks as he concentrates on driving.

Chapter 12
First Kill

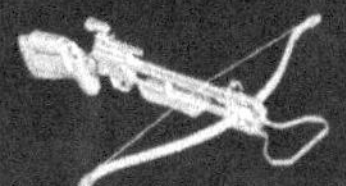

Scanning the horizon, I try to see why Jago brought us here. The man in question is slipping down the sand covered wall of the building we are perched in, with me lying down and keeping my eye out for any of those biker people again, or what Jago explained as clans people.

Biting my lip, I bring the sniper scope to my eye and scan the horizon, I was given a quick lesson on it, but I only really know how to look through the scope and shoot, and I have never actually hit anything, so here's hoping I don't need to.

I watch through my scope as he crouches and crawls across the sandy terrain, freezing every time he must hear something. I feel like I am holding my breath. I don't know why he picked this shack out of all the others, but he says he has a feeling and needs to check it out and as patrol, it's our job. Who knew, I thought it was just fucking and driving. Oops, did I mention that as soon as we got out of sight of Paradise, Jago pulled up behind a building and yanked me into the back seat and ravished me? Yeah, that boy is finnneee, even thinking about it now has my panties wet. Shit, pay attention Piper.

Grinning, I scan the horizon again before concentrating on his ass as he moves, oh yeah. He is fine alright. I have never been into older men before, but christ on a cracker, let's just say that ain't a problem anymore.

I go back to my scanning again, and something glints a little ways out and I focus on it, not breathing as I wait. It glints again. There is someone definitely there. Shit. Tilting the scope back to Jago I wait, how the fuck do I get his attention without firing? At this range I can't tell who it is and they might not be foe, plus it will draw the attention to whoever is around here. No, no shooting.

Think, Piper, fucking think. An idea comes to mind but I know Jago will kill me, well at least he will be alive. Moaning at my own stupidity, I drop the rifle over my shoulder using the strap, and climb down from my vantage point. Pulling my knife from my boot I set out to where I saw the glint.

There is no point crouching or trying to stay hidden, nothing but dust lies between me and it, so whoever is there will see me coming a mile off. Groaning, I decide to run, they might not expect that. Dodging dead trees and debris, I stop dead when I see the man waiting for me.

He is casually leaning back against a silver bike and he is fucking beautiful. His hair is blond and cut short, and he has the most beautiful blue eyes, deep and full, like the pictures of the ocean you were shown in lessons. His face is all angles and filled with a cold confidence. Even as I stare at him with a knife in my hand, he lounges like he is out here to get a tan. Tilting his head he grins at me, his eyes dropping to my body and slowly drinking me in. I shiver at the intensity as he meets my eyes again, his filled with heat.

"Hmm, I know what Dray means now," he says, grinning like I should know what that means. When I don't respond his grin stretches. "Not a talker?"

"Who are you?" I ask, gripping my knife tighter as sweat trickles down my temple. I am acutely aware that my back is open to an attack and it's making me nervous, and I am worried about leaving Jago when I should be watching his back.

"Name's not important, what is, is that your little boyfriend there is running into a hive of scavs. Scavs I am hunting, I don't like when others play with my toys."

I don't even know what the fuck to say to that. "You mean it's a trap?" I screech.

"Sort of, just not for you two." Sighing, he pushes away from his bike faster than I thought possible. "Come on then, let's go save your boyfriend." He swings onto his bike and pats the spot behind him. I debate my options before jumping on after him, my concern for Jago overriding everything.

Crinkling my nose I lean away. "You smell like shit," I comment and he grunts out what sounds like a laugh.

"You don't smell like roses, Princess." With that, he guns it, dust spraying in our wake and I have no choice but to grip him and hold on tight. He roars right up to the shack. Kicking the stand into place he slides from his bike, I have to jump off as he opens the door like he owns the joint.

Whistling, I peek over his shoulder to see Jago facing off with six rough looking men. "Hello boys, who wants to play?" he mocks, then slips into action.

I watch from the door, my knife clutched in my hand as he slips around the room, blood flowing in his wake as he kills them. He makes it look like art, the moves so fluid and clean, whereas Jago just rips them apart, all brutal and bloody. Not two minutes later they are both panting in the middle of the room, side by side, staring at me. Jago is covered in blood and his eyes are locked on mine with lust and anger. The newcomer looks amused and not a hair is out of place, the prick isn't even sweating.

"Behind you, Princess," he comments casually, and I swing around to see a big bastard trying for the newcomer's bike. Not wanting to get anywhere near him, I chuck the knife like Jago taught me, and it hits him in the back. He goes down with a scream, his hands reaching back to try and pull it out. Striding forward, I don't wait for them, wanting to prove I can look after myself and that I have listened to Jago's training.

When I reach him, I grab the knife, placing my foot on his back to wiggle it from his skin. Once done, I hack down into his exposed neck as he screams, not allowing myself to think of him as a person. I know he would kill me just as easily, I know he had tried to run, but he would go back and get others, they would find us and follow us back to Paradise—back to Evan.

I let that run through my head as blood spurts on me, and still I keep hacking until something warm and soft lands on my arms as I am about to swing again.

"He's dead," the newcomer murmurs, watching me, his eyes searching my face. When I nod and step back shakily, he lets go of my hand and I drop the knife to the ground, the blood with it, as my whole body shakes.

Oh god, I killed someone.

An arm wraps around my waist, turning me into a hard body and when the scent of Jago hits me, I bury my head into his chest. He drops his chin on top of my head and just holds me as a few tears escape, and I fight through my shock, this is what it is after all. I know Jago is watching the newcomer and not wanting to give much away, so I stay quiet as well until I feel more put together.

Once I do, I squeeze his arm and step back, he lets me as we face off with the newcomer. I watch with horror and interest as he crouches down and turns over the guy. I make sure not to look at his face as he searches his body.

"Good job, Princess," he says happily while searching the body, and I swallow my bile as I finally look into the dead man's empty eyes. The newcomer keeps talking, but I can't seem to look away from those dead eyes.

My eyes dart up as the newcomer stands, his head tilted as he watches me. He looks from me to the man on the floor, and a dawning sort of understanding crosses his face before he schools it. "He killed three whores at The Ring, and him and his buddies stole another two, raped and tortured 'em," he explains casually, and when it sinks in, some of the guilt of killing him evaporates and I know that was his intention, but why?

"Who are you?" I ask again, and he wags his finger.

"You have an obsession with names," he deflects, filling his bag with something.

"Oh yes, it's an obsession to want to know what to call someone instead of just asshole or cocky bastard," I joke and Jago grunts.

"Hmm, how about hero?" he counters, winking at me, and I arch my eyebrow.

"How about little dick?" I reply and laughter tumbles from him, and he watches me with growing interest. Jago interrupts by stepping halfway in front of me and facing off with the new guy.

"Why are you here?" Jago grumbles.

"For the view of course," the newcomer replies and I bite my lip. "He mentioned he was tracking them and we stepped into his trap," I add helpfully and he looks around Jago with a hurt expression.

"Woah, what a way to let a guy down. Betrayed at the first hurdle," he says dramatically and I just grin at him.

"You were tracking the scavs?" Jago asks, there's that word again. Scavs.

"Interesting," the new guy murmurs, and I look around Jago as he rights his bike and climbs up. "Yes, I was. Now if you don't fucking mind, I am going to collect my reward. Good luck Princess, don't let him rip you apart too bad." I open my mouth to let out a scathing reply, but he speeds away with a laugh. What an ass.

"He's right, I won't rip you up...too bad." Jago winks and strides into the house, and I am left gawking after him. What the monkey nuts just happened?

❧

We search the house quickly before Jago sighs and tells me it's time to get going, that the smell of blood and rot will start soon and will attract ferals. I follow after him and once we reach the truck, I go to walk around to the passenger side when he stops and spins me. My back hits the hot metal and he hikes my legs up, I wrap them around him automatically as his lips meet mine. He kisses me harshly, almost desperately, before pulling away and dropping his forehead to mine.

"Do you know how fucking terrified I was when I saw you appear in that doorway, the odds were bad enough that I was going to get the fuck out of there, and then you just fucking appear." I go to open my mouth when he drops another bruising kiss on my lips.

"I told you to fucking stay there, to watch my back." Another kiss. "Of course you didn't." Another.

Getting frustrated that he won't let me talk, I wrap my hands in his hair and yank his head back. He grunts, narrowing his eyes on mine, and I cover his mouth with my other hand.

"No, fucking listen. I am not a fucking damsel in distress. I didn't sign up for that shit, I get enough back there. You never hold back, you trust me to take the shit with the good and handle myself, so don't start questioning that now. Yes, I should have been up there but I saw something on the road, and not wanting to shoot to draw attention to us, I made a call. It might have been wrong but it doesn't fucking matter, I made it. Now, you are going to think carefully about your next words or I swear, you big cuntholio, I will never touch your special place again." I huff, glaring at him. Trying to act indignant while being pinned to a car like a five year old is hard, but I totally nail it.

I lift my hand slowly and he licks his lips and blows out a breath, his eyes watching me. "You are right," he grits out and I grin.

"Huh, how did that taste?" I ask sweetly, knowing how much it will have pained him to say that.

"Like fucking shit, but you are right."

I lean forward and kiss his lips in thanks, and he smiles as I pull away. "We need to work on your reaction times and teach you some hand-to-hand if you plan on rushing in," he adds, a smirk on his face as I groan. Of course the sick bastard turns this back to training

"You know, I think you just use training as an excuse to feel me up," I say snottily, and he leans forward, licking my lips as he whispers against them.

"And your point is?"

I groan and chase after him, but he drops me to the floor and walks away.

"You owe me at least two orgasms for that shit!" I call, and slide inside as he starts laughing. Men, you can't live with them, and you sure as shit can't make them give you orgasms during training it seems. One day.

Chapter 13
Forgotten Pain

The rest of patrol is boring, as we follow the route, keeping our eyes peeled. Jago explains a bit more about the clans and what scavs are, and I listen intently. From the way the elders in Paradise speak, I never guessed there were this many people left out here, and if they knew then why don't they help them? Or slowly bring us back into the world?

"I don't know, all I know is that out here...it's another life entirely. I don't think the people of Paradise would survive. It's so..." "Brutal," I finish, the man's face I killed earlier flashing in my head, even knowing what he did doesn't make it better. I think this is just something you have to live with.

"The first time is always the hardest," he mutters softly and I glance over at him, hanging onto his words like a lifeline so I don't go back into my own mind and relive that moment again and again, like I have found myself doing all night.

"Is it? Was yours?" I ask, almost desperately.

He sighs, his hands tightening on the wheel. "Yes, I still remember the look on his face. The feel of his blood on my hands, the panic, and how fucking glad I was to be alive."

I stare at him as he speaks and I see the truth on his face. That death, whoever the man was, still haunts him. "Will it be like that for me?" I question, not wanting to see that man every time I sleep.

"No," he grunts, not looking at me.

"Why is it for you?" I press softly, knowing I am pushing and he might just shut down.

"Because he was my father," he spits out and I swallow hard, watching his face shut down as his eyes lock on the road.

I don't know what to say, so I reach over and squeeze his arm, but he doesn't react so I look back out my window, concentrating on patrol and trying to ignore the frosty atmosphere. The man's face flashes in my mind again, the feeling of his warm blood seeping through my fingers as his eyes dim and his mouth opens, blaming me for his death.

"What happened?" The words slip out and I wince, I can tell he doesn't want to talk but I need to, to distract myself, lose myself in his words, even his anger.

"Drop it," he warns, his voice colder than ever.

Desperation claws at me, I need him now more than ever. "Come on, I told you mine, tell me yours," I choke out and he slams on the breaks.

"I said fucking drop it, what the fuck is wrong with you?" he snarls and I rock back like he has smacked me. "Fuck, I forgot how immature you are."

He turns to face the front as I swallow hard, looking away from him as tears well in my eyes. Breathing through it, I ignore him.

The rest of patrol is spent in near silence, only trading terse words when necessary. He is pulling away from me and I let him, knowing that I caused it, and he is relieving the pain. I know that better than anyone.

I go to speak so many times only to bite my lip.

At the end of patrol we return to Paradise, the mood so somber compared to our way out. Once inside the bunker he slams the car door shut, making me jump, and without bothering to unload the truck, stalks away, ignoring the questioning looks.

I know he needs some time alone to push back his demons, I am the same way, but it hurts that he felt he couldn't tell me that. Sighing, I push from the car and unpack. It takes twice as long, and I am covered in sweat and swaying from exhaustion when I'm done. Not wanting to leave anything for Jago to do, I go check us back in and answer all the questions, telling them he has gone to medical. They nods and accept this, waving me away.

Tired, mardy, and a little bit pissed with myself, I make my way back to my room. I really don't want to be alone but everyone else are just people I hang with when I am bored, and it doesn't really appeal to me right now. When I reach my door, I find Evan lifting his hand to knock.

"Evan?" I call out, and my voice sounds funny even to me. Wrapping my arms around my waist I watch as he turns, his face cold and his eyes are looking at everything but me. Just another thing I ruined.

It's like seeing him opens the dam and I want to cry, I want to scream, I want to hide in his arms like that scared ten-year-old girl again. I want him and he won't even look at me. I thought I was through having my heart broken by him, I was wrong.

"Just wanted to see if you were okay," he mutters, barely glancing at me. If he did, he would see how lost and alone I was. How much my heart is hurting and how hard I am fighting to keep the tears at bay. I took a man's life today, I want to scream it at him. Beg him to take the memory away, as even now dead eyes flash in my mind and I have to swallow a scream.

Please, Evan...Evvie. Make it stop.

But of course he doesn't. I nod and he turns, and without a word he leaves. I watch him brokenly, my arms the only thing holding me together.

As soon as he rounds the corner I gasp out a breath, trembling as the tears track down my face. "Please, please don't leave me alone with nothing but...that memory," I whisper, hoping he will turn back. Hoping he will notice how much I am suffering. He doesn't.

Stumbling through the door, I slide down the floor with my back to the wall. The bed is still mussed from Jago and me, and I have to bite my lip at that. I wish he was here as well, to hold me in his big arms and make everything better. I wish they both were.

Laying my head back against the wall, I try to slow my breathing. Closing my eyes I draw up the memory of my mum, her smiling face as she tucked me in that last time and sang to me.

"Oh, my sweet, sweet girl. The sun will shine and the skies will cry, oh my sweet sweet girl. High you soar, on the wings above. Oh my sweet sweet girl. Love, you are love."

A sob bursts out of me and I bury my head into my knees, crying for everything I have lost, and everything I have to lose. I stay locked like that for a while before I push myself from the floor, strip- ping as I go, finally needing to get the blood off of me.

In the shower I scrub until my skin is pink. I have to force myself not to keep scrubbing. I break down again, curling in the cold water at the bottom and holding myself, feeling like if I don't I will break into pieces and drift down the drain with the water. It's strange, now that the shock has worn off, all I can feel is the horror and like Jago said—the relief that I am alive. I was reminded today how fragile life is and how easy it can be snuffed out, and it brings all my pain and heartache from losing my parents to the surface.

Dragging myself up, I dry off quickly before dropping into bed, and close my eyes. Sleep doesn't come easily and when it does, it's filled with empty eyes and bloodied sand. By morning my eyes are stinging and I am more tired than I was yesterday. Determined not to be broken, I struggle from bed and get dressed.

Happy that I have enough time, I make my way to the dining room and grab some coffee from the earlier morning server. Keeping my head down I head to the gym, and when I get there it is still locked but I am early, so I sit on the floor and nurse my coffee and wait.

He turns up five minutes late looking as shitty as I feel. He doesn't even speak to me and I can't seem to force the words past my lips.

Following him in, I throw away my coffee and warm up as he sets out the mats, my eyes flicking back to him. When he is done he waits for me, his eyes not meeting mine, and I sigh before standing opposite him.

"Jago—" I start but he cuts me off by running at me. I manage to side step him, just.

He comes at me again and again, not giving me time to talk, never mind think, as everything narrows down to avoiding his fists and kicks. One sneaks past and winds me, another knocks me on my ass and I start to get mad. Jumping up I run at him with a yell.

He was the one who took me out there.

He was the one who brought up the conversation. He was the one who left when I needed him.

I let it take over, hitting harder and moving faster as I spit venomous words at him in my head. I land a punch, then another, until we are fighting for real. Neither of us holding back.

His head snaps to the side and we both freeze, I see blood running from his lip and he steps back. "Good."

I open my mouth but he grabs his stuff and leaves me there, bewildered and still pissed.

Screaming, I spin and take my anger out on the punching bag before running laps. I am a sweaty exhausted mess when the others start trickling in to use the gym. I get some funny looks but luckily no one tries to speak to me as I grab my shit and leave. I storm back to my room and take a quick shower, as a plan forms in my head. If I leave it to fester, this shit between us will just grow. I am going to confront the beast.

I have spent the last two hours hunting around this god forsaken maze and still no Jago. I spot Todd heading from practice and corner him, and he reluctantly tells me where Jago's place is. Grinning, I start to jog away and I turn backwards to face him, yelling out, "Thanks again, nice balls!" I shout just in time for some guards to leave the gym. Laughing to myself I follow Todd's instructions, more determined than ever, my pity party fully over. So I killed a guy, yes that shit is horrible, yes I have to live with that, but I can't let that stop me, not now. And yes we said some words in anger, but I know I pushed him too far.

I find his place after ten minutes and I knock three times. Eventually I hear him swear before the door slides open, revealing an infuriated Jago, his mouth open, probably ready to tear me a new one, and he freezes when he sees me and snaps it shut again

"What do you want?" he growls, blocking the door.

"I came to apologise, I am sorry for pushing you earlier. That wasn't cool, it's just—" I blow out a breath and I see his eyes soften for a moment.

"You shouldn't be here, Brawler."

"Jago, please. I just wanted to apologise. I shouldn't have brought up your father when you clearly didn't want to talk about it," I plead and I know I said the wrong thing when his face shuts down.

"You are going on patrol with Team C tonight," he says and I grit my teeth.

"Fine." Swiveling on my heel I march away, I'm not fighting with him all night. It is clear he is pushing me away. If he wants to be like that when I opened up to him, fine. I will accept his apology in the form of orgasms when he comes back.

I grab my stuff from my room and make my way to the hangar, not wanting to be late and wanting to meet Team C. I've met B and a few others, but the name doesn't ring a bell. When I get there I spot the C on a side of a truck and make my way over, only to stop when I see who else is there.

Oh fuck no.

"Well, well, well, slut. This should be fun," Eel jokes, grinning at me.

Chapter 14
C Stands for Cunt

Ignoring Eel, I throw my pack in the back of the car and lean against it, waiting for whoever else is in the team to arrive. Eel slides up next to me, so close we are touching.

"Ready to have some fun?" He reaches out to stroke my arm and I decide to end this shit right now. Grabbing the offending limb, I twist it like Jago showed me and push his face into the side of the truck.

"Listen up dickwad, just because your mum should have swallowed you doesn't mean you get to be an insufferable cunt. You don't get to touch me, and if you do it again I will break your little nose. We have a job to do, if you don't think you can do that with a woman on your team, tuck up your cock and run back to your mum." I push him harder and he grunts, wiggling to try and get away. "Understand?" I ask and he yelps when I press harder.

"Yes!" he finally shouts and I let go, stepping back and waiting in case he decides to attack. By the looks of it, the 'C' in C Team stands for cunts, let's hope the rest of them are better.

He spins, fury on his face, and I know he is going to attack when laughter and clapping sounds from around us, and I glance to see the whole hangar has stopped to watch. Eel's face heats and he steps back, but I see the look in his eyes, and I know he wants revenge. I run my gaze over the crowd again and my eyes lock with Jago's where he stands off to the side, he nods before striding away and I have the urge to run after him, but instead I sigh and lean back against the truck as two more men turn up. A little bit taller than me and packing some serious muscle, they look like nearly every other patrol or guard. They aren't unattractive, but compared to Jago and even Evan, they are. One, who introduces himself as Ilo has dull brown eyes and flat blond hair. The other, Newt, has sparkling green eyes but the rest of his face is forgettable. By the swagger in their walk and the confidence coating their bodies, they think they are god's gifts, but they are pleasant enough to me so I relax a little.

They shake my hand and laugh, ignoring Eel altogether. I nod in the appropriate places and try to keep my lips sealed, needing to make this work. We pack up quickly and I jump in the back with Newt, as Ilo takes the driver's seat and Eel takes the passenger seat. They share a few looks and that's when I remember that Eel has been out with them before. So they obviously know him. An uneasy feeling starts in my stomach, but I push it away and return Ilo's kind smile.

"Ready?" he asks, looking in the mirror at us in the back.

"Yep," I reply, trying to stay cheerful, but I am not nearly as excited about this patrol as I usually am, and I blame that sexy, angry bastard lurking somewhere in the other side of the hangar.

Patrol is boring, and it's not just the sex I am missing...well, not all of it. What makes it even more boring and strange is how Newt, Ilo, and Eel all ignore me after we leave the hangar. They don't even let me map read or scout, it's obvious to them I am a burden and besides the few searching looks, and the worst ones, lust filled, I stay quiet in my seat in the back.

They throw me looks every so often and when they pull up to

check a house in their sector, a rundown two story one which I am amazed it is still standing, I go to leave the truck only for Newt in the seat next to me to grab my arm. It feels like ants are crawling from his touch and I shiver at the disgusting feeling. I don't know why, but I really don't want him touching me. Weird because he seems okay, nice enough, even if he is sexist. But as a woman, I think we all have this internal radar that throws warnings out around certain people, it might just be a feeling, but they tend to be right. Your soul knows, even when your mind doesn't, that it's a man you should stay away from.

I gently pull away but he keeps his hold, making me grit my teeth. "Stay in the truck, keep your eyes out," he demands before letting go and slipping out to join the others. Flexing my arm, I eye the red handprint he left before looking out the window, that bad feeling still churning in my gut. They walk towards the house, nudging and laughing with each other, which only makes me frown harder.

Okay Piper, you know you have to get on with these guys. Just bite your lip and get through tonight. You can make up with Jago and be back on normal patrols. Plan sorted, I sit up straighter in my seat, turning slightly to the side so I can keep them in my line of sight when they return. I even clutch my katana that Jago gave me closer.

They come back after ten minutes, looking mighty pleased with themselves and that uneasy feeling only kicks up a notch. They eye me and nod at each other before taking their seats back in the truck.

"Everything okay?" I force myself to ask.

Newt looks over, grinning in what I am guessing is supposed to be a reassuring way, but I want to scream and jump from the truck which just started up. "Everything's fine, it was empty inside so we will carry on with patrol."

I nod and turn back to face the front, even as I feel him eyeing me. They seem nice enough, so why can't I get rid of this feeling?

"That big bastard, what's his name...Beast, your boyfriend?" he questions, leaning closer like it's a secret even though I see Eel and Ilo twitch in the front, obviously eavesdropping. The way he said Beast puts me on edge, like an insult instead of the respect that man deserves, even when he's being a wanker.

I hesitate, wanting to say yes so it would put them off, but that will only increase the rumours and I don't think Jago would appreciate it much. "No," I reply tersely.

"You hear that Eel? Looks like you were wrong," he jokes, and I grit my teeth and block out their banter.

I spend the rest of patrol splitting my time between looking at them and then out of the window. Compared to Jago they are sloppy, they wouldn't even notice if anyone snuck up on us, never mind if we actually got in a real fight. When the sun starts to rise again and we head back to Paradise I breathe a little bit easier, and when we roll through the bunker door I quickly leave the vehicle. My skin is still crawling as I feel them stare at me.

I spot Jago in his usual bay and ignoring anyone else, make way over there. Fuck this stupid fight. When I reach his truck I lean on the side as he unpacks.

"Hey," I say softly, and he jerks his head up, obviously not hearing me walk over which is strange.

"Hi," he grunts, turning back to his stuff.

"Look I'm sorry, we both said and did stupid shit. Let's just forget it all and get back to our 'I give you shit you pretend not to love it' dynamic," I tease and he snorts, but he still doesn't look at me.

"Jago?" I ask, stepping closer.

He sighs, staring down at the bag in his truck.

"I am being pulled from patrol for three nights, I have to go with a crew for a run."

"What for?" I inquire, disappointment clouding my judgment, I want to reach out but I can't with us being in public.

"Just a mission, you will stay with Team C and when I get back you will join me again," he explains and I see him search my eyes. I nod and we stare at each other, both having so much to say but not knowing how to say it.

"Beast, let's go!" comes a yell and he sighs.

With another nod he turns and walks away, but watching him makes my heart ache, so I turn away and slide behind the truck. Slumping there I frown at the ground until with a gasp, I am pushed back into it.

Lips cover mine, the taste familiar, and I close my eyes in bliss. It's over too soon and when my lashes flutter open, I see Jago walking away again.

Men.

Chapter 15
The Last Goodbye

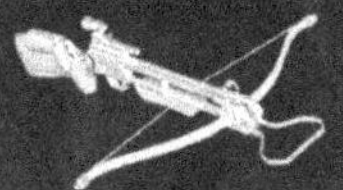

After he walks away, I slump back over to C Team and grab my stuff from the truck, while trying to ignore the tingling in my lips. That man is way too fine for his own good.

"Where are you going? Don't you want to party with us?" Dickwad, aka Eel, sneers as he leans back against the truck, watching me.

Flipping him off, I leave and sign myself back in, showing my bag to security. With nothing—or no one—else to do, I head back to my room to shower off the sand and dust.

Dropping my bag at the door, I strip on my way and take a quick shower. I dry off and head back into my room, and then get dressed again. This time in stretchy pants and a tank top. I'm too wound up to sleep and I don't know why. There is that stupid fucking lump in my stomach. Maybe I'm worried for Jago, or maybe I'm missing Evan, but I'm not exactly good at feelings and shit.

So, instead, I head to the cafeteria and sweet talk the guy there into giving me cake. Not the kind you would find from before, it's a replica, but it still tastes damn good, maybe because I don't have anything to compare it to. Swinging my legs on the worktop in the kitchen I eat it in peace, watching him and his crewmate as they prepare breakfast for everyone.

When people start shuffling in for breakfast I make myself scarce, and with nowhere else to go I find myself back in the place it all started. The room I made out with Todd in. Sighing, I sit down and let my mind wander.

I'm so lost in my own thoughts that I don't even notice the door open and someone come in until he sits next to me.

Blinking, I stare at the side of Evan's face in confusion. When he doesn't speak, I stare back at the wall, refusing to play games. I'm mardy and pissed off, it's not a good combination.

"You okay?" he asks, and it's the same question he has been asking every day since I started patrols. Usually the only words he speaks to me. I know if I say yes he will get up and walk away, and that will be the end of our interaction for tonight.

"No." I force the word out between clenched teeth, still staring stubbornly at the wall.

His breath hitches and I can feel him staring at me. "What happened?" he growls, all hint of self-pity and frost melting from his voice to be replaced with my usual Evvie. It causes a horrible laugh to tumble from my throat. I really have to verbally tell him that I am not okay for him to even look at me now? And people say women are the weaker sex.

"Someone hurt you? Who do I have to kill? Pip, you fucking talk to me right now!"

I hear the panic as he yells and it sobers up my laughter. I look over at him and his face drops from the look in my eyes. "Today I spent the day with three assholes who I am pretty sure were more bothered about my vagina than protecting Paradise. Jago, the only person who believed in me when I started this, has gone away, leaving me to try and protect myself against all the fucking misogynistic assholes out there, and you. You hurt me, you tossed me aside like I was nothing to you. Like I didn't spend all my life loving you. You walked away like I was nothing when I have supported you every day of your life. All I needed was you, even if you didn't like my choices it didn't matter to me so long as you were there, and then you weren't. I was left alone again, like when my parents died. Then you ask me if I'm okay?" I snort out a bitter laugh. "I lost my best friend, the boy I am in love with." I stop as he sucks in a breath and I smile sadly. "Was in love with." I see the moment the words register. This time I am going to be the one to walk away, because this back and forth game is killing me, maybe I just needed to get this all out. "At least have the balls to walk away completely, because this...distance is killing me. I can't do it. You need to decide what you want Evan, but don't be surprised if I'm not there when you do."

I can't help it, maybe it's because I know I am finally saying good-bye, or that I need to know just once what it feels like, but I lean forward and kiss him. Hate, hurt, and shared pasts swirl between us. He leans into me almost desperately, tasting me, grip- ping my face as if to keep me here with him.

I groan into his mouth, tangling my tongue with his as I show him exactly how much I loved him. Then I pull away. While he sits there, looking dazed with his eyes closed, I lean closer again and kiss him softly. "Goodbye, Evvie."

Getting up, I walk away knowing that it might have hurt, but it is the right decision.

I sleep hard, that deep kind that only happens after something big happens in your life. When I wake up, I feel good. I know where I stand with Jago and now with Evan, and although I have to put up with the three twats for three nights, I know after that I will be back with Jago and we will fall into a routine again.

Getting up slowly, I make sure to stretch out my body. I'm not bothering to head into the gym, there isn't really time anyway. Instead, I take a shower, a long leisurely one. I scrub at my skin and shave, and even condition my hair. It makes me feel better, and when

I step out into the steam with a towel wrapped around me, I feel like a new woman. Slightly dramatic, but I can roll with it.

I tug on my black skinny jeans and a tank top, laying my jacket out on the bed. I even pull out the katana and the strap, which mysteriously appeared in my room yesterday. It slips over my shoulder and lies perfectly along my spine. Slipping into it, I prac- tice again, pulling out the sword and sheathing it over my shoulder. It takes some skill, and the first time I did it I smacked myself in the face with the pummel of the sword. The next time, I fell over. Don't ask how, even I'm not sure. It's still not a smooth, refined movement—I don't know how all those people in films make it look easy—but at least I no longer look like a turtle on its back. I even look more badass, wait...is that the right word? Baddasser, badass extraordinaire? Ah fuck it, who knows. Either way, I look like I can kick ass.

I need to practice more with Janet—yes, I called my sword Janet. It's like one of those old bitchy women down here that always goes straight for the throat and gets blood—get it? So Janet it is. Anyway, I need to practice more but I think I could take on some attackers if need be. It makes me feel better, especially after I realised last night that C Team doesn't give a flying monkey fuck whether I live or die.

Glancing at the clock I sigh in defeat. I slip off the sheath and grab my jacket, before making my way to the hangar. One night, that's all I need to make it through with these morons before I can be back at Jago's side.

Easy enough, right?

Chapter 16
Left For Dead

The C Team are already waiting when I reach the hangar. Squaring my shoulders I head their way. As usual, they start whispering between themselves and throwing me looks, ignoring them like the gossiping pussies they are, I start loading up the truck.

A throat clearing behind me has me straightening and turning to see the Captain, the one who was rude to me and Jago the other day. Turns out that prick is in charge of all patrols and guards.

"I just wanted to wish you luck tonight," he says, but his tone is frosty, and when his eyes slip to the men who suddenly appear at my side I shiver.

"Oh, don't worry Captain. We will make sure she does," Eel sneers and the Captain nods, his lips twitching ever so slightly.

Shaking off the bad feeling, I nod my head. Without even looking at me the Captain wanders away, checking over other teams and moving through the hangar. What the hell was that about? He's always been a giant cuntasarusrex to me, plus I'm pretty sure he hates women, but that was just weird. Blowing out a breath, I finish packing the truck while trying to ignore the bad feeling curling in the pit of my stomach. It's not like I can bow out of tonight's patrol. I fought to get this spot, and I can't keep depending on Jago to protect me and have my back. I will just have to make sure I have my own.

"Let's roll!" I hear one of them shout, so I quickly finishing packing the back and slam the door shut, then make my way to the back seat.

"You're up front today!" comes a call, and when I peer over the roof to see Newt staring at me. Nodding, I slide in the front passenger seat, fidgeting from having Eel and Ilo behind me. Turning slightly, so my back is to the door, I raise my knee and look out of the front window. I don't know why I'm so jittery tonight, but it's going to be a long patrol if I let it get to me. So ignoring it, I watch as the hangar door rolls up and the alarm blares.

We are the third to leave tonight, and when we break through into the sand I draw in a deep breath. I wonder what tonight's patrol holds?

～

For the first hour, it's pretty boring. We rove our sector, and the guys occasionally get out to take a leak or investigate some- thing, but all seems quiet so they decide to head farther into the Wastes, away from our zone. It's getting late, it will be dark in a couple of hours but I don't bother pointing that out, it would only piss them off further.

We just get deeper and deeper into unknown territory and I start to fidget, but then we pull over. Looking around, I spot nothing that could have drawn their attention. Frowning, I turn around to ask what we are doing but a hand grabs my arm, hard. I know something isn't right, this isn't the usual patrol route and when they flick off the radio in the truck, I slide closer to the door. I had a bad feeling, hell, Jago had a bad feeling, and I think I am about to be proved right.

"Get out and check the boot, will ya? I think it might be open from when we stopped last time," Newt tells me, and I nod and break away from his grip. Better to be outside and in the open then stuck inside the truck with those three and the vibe they are throwing off.

Kicking open my door, I slide out and slam it shut in their faces. Making my way around the car, I stop at the closed boot. Seriously, what the fuck is going on? I hear doors open and shut as they round the car, coming to me.

Backing away from the boot, I give myself room to move. I only spot Newt and Ilo though, and for every step I take back, they step forward.

"What's going on? We should head back to our route before it gets dark," I suggest hesitantly, but when they share a grin and turn lust filled eyes back on me, I start to panic.

I feel the hair on the back of my neck stand up just as someone breathes on me and whispers in my ear, "Boo."

I go down hard when a fist smashes into the side of my head unexpectedly. It's the opening they need, and all three of them are on me faster than I can blink my dazed eyes open.

The sand heats my back as I flail and kick, trying to keep them off me. My sword is trapped under me and I couldn't get it if I tried, but I do have a dagger slipped into my boot, I just need to get it. Holding my arm up, I block the blows raining down on my face as I try to get to my feet. It's no use, there are too many of them. Someone grabs my hand and pins it to the sand, as another knocks away the one protecting my face and smashes a fist into my nose.

I hear a crack and I start coughing as blood trickles down the back of my throat. My other hand is pinned above my head as someone leans over my kicking legs. I hear a grunt when I make impact, but within minutes they have me pinned beneath them—helpless.

Panic claws at my throat as my heart tries to break through my chest, a sick feeling starts in my stomach and tears gather in my eyes, but I refuse to let them show. I need to reason with them, I need to give them a motive to stop.

"Don't, you hurt me and you know you will get into trouble," I warn, my voice shaking.

They laugh as Eel's face looms over mine, blocking my view of the setting sun. "No we won't, you really think the Captain gives a fuck what we do to you...or better yet, that he didn't order this?"

"What?" I gasp, shock settling into my bones as fear blooms in my chest.

"Oh, how cute. You thought they would let you join patrol? No, you are a warning. A tragic attack tonight sees you dead, but they didn't say we couldn't have our fun first." He laughs as the others do.

My ears ring as my eyes blur, they planned this? My own people, the Captain, the person who is meant to protect us all, planned for them to kill me? Betrayal surges through me, but so does anger, and I start bucking beneath them as their hands wander along my body.

"Get the fuck off me! He'll kill you, Jago will kill you!" I scream, truth ringing in every word.

"He can try," one of them sneers.

I try to get their hands off me, but it's no use. I'm not strong enough to lift them off me, or even free my hands. Turning in their grip, I claw into their hands with my nails. I hear one of them swear before a slap throws my head sideways.

I taste sand and blood, but my attention is drawn away from the throbbing in my cheek and nose when someone rips away my tank top. Crying out, I start bucking again, like a mad woman as warm air hits my now bare stomach and chest. Next, they cut through my bra, and tears finally burst from my eyes as my nipples tighten in the cool breeze.

No, no, no. This isn't happening. It can't be.

I beg and plead with them. I fight them, but it doesn't make much difference. They laugh and sneer, their rude comments making me choke on my own sobs as they run their hands down my body. Tweaking my nipples and slapping my breasts.

Lifting my head, I cry out as I watch one of them unbutton my jeans. Twisting, I throw myself to the side but they just pin me down harder.

"Looks like she still has a little fight left in her, I say we fuck it out," Eel jokes and my blood turns cold.

I guess some part of me thought they would stop, that is all a sick joke or maybe that someone would come and save me, but this is the real world. Bad things happen to good people, nightmares are real and even as you plead to the sky, no one comes to save you.

When my cries and begging starts to annoy them, one of them backhands me hard. My neck jerks to the side as I taste sand again. My vision starts to dot as they drag my jeans down my legs even as I kick and writhe. They get it over my shoes on one foot and leave the other leg wrapped in my own jeans like a vice.

They rip away my underwear as I shake my head, blood, snot, and tears dripping down my face as I beg one more time.

"Please, I'll do anything!" I cry out, my voice hoarse.

"Oh, you will. Don't you worry," Eel promises, and when I lift my head again I watch in horror as his fingers squirm between my thighs, which I keep closed, all my effort focused on that. He manages to pry them open and one of the other guys holds my legs spread-eagle as the other moves up and pins my arms above my head.

His warm, sweaty fingers touch me, and I scream. I scream as he plays with my body, my throat sore and bleeding, but I don't stop. Needing a way to let out my horror and pain.

"Shut her up, will you?" Eel orders as he sticks a finger inside me, making me whimper.

My head gets slammed back into the dirt, again and again until I know I'm not screaming anymore. Dazed, I lay there limp as I feel him line up at my abused self. I have no more energy, no more fight. Nothing I do makes a difference, so instead I annoy them further, hoping they will knock me out. Fuck, anything just so I don't have to feel it.

Eel starts to push in and I scream again. "Fuck, shut her up!" he shouts, and the one at my hands grabs my head in a vice-like grip, and starts slamming it into the hard ground again.

Blackness begins to crawl across my vision as I feel him thrust fully inside me, ripping me. The last thing I see is his face twisted in pleasure as he uses my body.

Agony tearing through my body brings me gasping awake, my eyes blur as I try to concentrate on what's happening. My whole body aches, but when I blink rapidly I cry at the man above me.

Forcing myself to slip back into the abyss, I leave my body once again.

It feels like I float there, in between. I can feel my body and what is happening, but the darkness cushions me and I can't seem to care—I can't seem to feel anything.

Eventually I come back to my body, and I wished I hadn't. Every inch of me hurts and feels violated. Stickiness coats my thighs and tears drip down my cheeks at what happened to me. Blood drips down my face as well, and when I glance down I notice it covers most of my body. It's clear they had their fun with me.

Resignation and hate build in me, blocking out everything and anything. I can hear the men packing up and laughing, but every time I move my body protests, so I lay here, in the sand, with blood and semen trickling down my bare thighs and tears streaming from my eyes. I want to sob, I want to scream. But I did that already and they just laughed. I knew these men, I saw them every day, some I trained with, but I trusted them all. How could they do this to me?

When the first growl reaches me I barely lift my head, but when I hear a blood-curdling scream I struggle into a sitting position, gasping when pain shoots through my whole body. My eyes widen in fear, and my heart starts to hammer again. I heard the stories about them, the cannibals, but I never believed them until now. Is it wrong that a part of me is happy?

One of them is ripping into Eel as he screams and begs the others to help him. Only they are busy fending off four more. It's obvious they didn't hear them creep up, because their guns are still on their packs to the left, and all they have is the few weapons strapped to their bodies. I watch in a detached sort of amusement as they fall. One after the other, each taken down by a living, growling monster.

They rip C Team to pieces, their screams splitting the air as the sound of them being eaten alive reaches me. The men manage to take a few with them though, I will give them that. Tilting my head I eye the creatures in fascination. I should be panicking, but I can't seem to bring myself to care anymore. They look human, but almost skeletal. Their bodies are thin and malnourished, with bones sticking through their paper-thin skin which is almost yellow and hard like leather, obviously from being under the sun. Straggly unwashed hair covers one of the creature's heads, while the others are bald. Their faces look misshapen, their mouths covered in blood, but I can spot the sharp looking teeth. They are more monster than man.

Trying to keep silent, I know I need to move before they spot me. So I struggle to my feet only to fall back on my ass with a scream, as white-hot agony spreads through my body. In dawning horror I watch as one of the cannibal's head snaps up and it's soulless eyes lock onto me, and that's when I realise. I do care. I don't want to die here.

No, no, no. I didn't survive those bastards to be eaten alive. Grabbing anything behind me I pull myself away, since its obvious I can't stand yet. Those bastards royally fucked me up, so I drag myself like an animal, crying and hiccupping as the hot sand burns my naked ass and legs. I hit a rock with my left thigh and cry out when I feel it puncture my skin, but I still keep going. The cannibal watches me the whole time, before jumping forward on all fours and sniffing at the sand.

Oh god, when I look at where it's smelling, I notice I am leaving a trail of blood after me. Eyes still on me, it leans down and licks it before licking its lips and growling. My stomach revolts and I have to turn to the side to be sick. My sweaty, messy hair sticks to my damp face and neck, and I quickly wipe my mouth on the back of my arm. Looking back I notice it has crawled forward, it's arse in the air like some kind of old-world dog as it hunts me.

"No," I cry out, my voice still rough and hoarse from screaming. Looking around for anything to use as a weapon, I panic when I spot nothing. With renewed vigor, ignoring the pain with every movement, I drag myself back, faster and faster, but it's no use. It's on me within one minute, obviously done toying with me.

I freeze when it sniffs at my foot and makes it twitch, holding my breath, like it might just disappear if I don't look. But I know that's not true.

It moves up my legs, licking a path through the dirt and blood with its blood stained tongue. When it opens its mouth wide, I see that its teeth have been filed into points, and bits of muscle and skin are stuck between them. I have to breathe shallowly to keep the bile down.

Think, Piper. Think. What would Jago do?

I feel my body weakening and my head is pounding. I know I don't have much longer, but I refuse to be made into cannibal chow. I'm losing too much blood from what those animals did to me, and from the stone still stuck in my thigh—*that's it!*

With nothing else to use, I reach down slowly and feel around the side of my thigh. My fingers slip in my own blood, but when I feel the jagged rock I have to breathe deep. Fuck, why does looking at it and feeling it suddenly make it real?

This is going to hurt, I think before locking my eyes with the cannibal and pulling with all the strength left in my broken and abused body. I bite through my lip, but the scream slips out anyway as the rock cuts through my leg. Panting and with shaking hands, I hold it up in front of me. As far as weapons go, it's not ideal, but it's something. Its head lowers as it growls again and I know it's getting prepared to leap at me. Fuck, fuckity fuck. Here goes nothing. I freeze, and when it launches through the air I thrust my rock up with a battle cry, loud enough to startle the nearby crows. Falling back to the sand I hardly breathe, my eyes still locked with its— there is nothing human there, not anymore—and when the life slowly drains from them I look down, and spot the rock protruding from deep within its chest.

With a disgusted cry I push and kick until the body falls to the side with a thump. Leaning back I let out a hysterical laugh. One down, one to go. The other one comes at me with a roar and I know I am too weak to take it, but I will go down fighting.

I blink in astonishment when a man, dressed all in black—including a hood covering his face—appears behind and slits its throat. It stumbles and falls down, the blood pooling around it just short of my feet. Looking up I pant hard, trying to fight off the blackness encroaching my vision again.

He watches me, not moving, and I know I am still not safe. Jago will kill me if I don't get up. Gritting my teeth I get to my knees, breathing deeply as I slowly get to my feet, stumbling a little. Suddenly the guy in the hood is there, holding me upright. I try to jerk away but he holds tight until I am steady, then steps back. My cheeks heat in shame but I refuse to let the tears fall as I reach down, whimpering at the pain in my body, and pull up my pants up my abused thighs. When I manage to get them up again I glance over to see him still watching me. "Thank you," I whisper, my throat raw and broken.

He nods, still not speaking, and steps back. Turning to the side I eye the car. Blood covers the hood and with a wince, I realise the hood is up and at least two tires are flat. I wonder if it will still run after the damage it took. Pulling in a breath, I sway as I turn lightheaded.

I need to get somewhere safe, and fast. I should head back, Jago will be worried sick, but then it also means I would be in more danger and I will put him at risk. No, I can't do that. They wanted me dead, they won't stop, not now. I know too much, they can't allow it. They will use him and Evan to get to me, it's better if I disappear until I am healed, and then think of a new plan.

Something warm and faintly smelling like fire lands on my shoulders. I whirl, the black cloak slipping down my shoulders, but the man is gone, all that is left is his cloak. I shiver at the thought, I can almost feel him watching me, but I tug it closed to cover my exposed skin. It's a testament to how injured I am that I forgot about being shirtless. Looking down I spot a rifle to the side and grab it.

Standing, using the rifle as a walking stick, I look at the two directions. I could go west, back to Paradise and Evan and Jago, it's where my heart wants to go. I am in desperate need of their comfort and to cry out my pain, but how do I know I won't be killed on sight? I'm betting I have been reported as dead by now, and who is going to believe a lowly patrol over a Captain? Evan would, but at this point I don't know if that means much. To the east I at least have a chance, a slim chance. I'm bleeding badly with only a bottle of water and the rest of the guys' supplies to get me somewhere, but it's better, it has to be, right?

Glancing a final time in the direction of Paradise, I turn without a backwards glance. My heart stutters and tries to pull me back, but I know there is nothing left for me there. How could I go back to that place of monsters? At least out here I know who they are. I leave the car behind, making it look like they were attacked and I was taken, and I remind myself it is better this way. It's not goodbye forever, just for now. Until I have a plan, then I go back for my men.

Chapter 17
Being Alive Hurts

The sun beats down on me. My whole body is sweating and hurting like an open wound. I don't even know how I keep moving, putting one foot in front of the other. It's the only thing I concentrate on. I know I must be delirious at this point, no water plus this much trauma messing with me so even the world seems to tilt. Oh wait, nope, that's just me falling.

I land on the sand with a thump, a pained cry slipping from my cracked lips. Shaking my head I crawl to my feet, determined to keep going, but only one step later I fall again. My body doesn't want to move this time, no matter how loud I scream in my own head.

The sky is orange, the night peeking through as I stare at it helplessly. I am going to die here. It's my only thought as reality swims and mixes with the blackness trying to claim me.

"I've got you," comes a deep, familiar voice.

Looking up I meet the eyes of the man who fought by Jago's side in that hut, the man I killed in front of. He smells like the hood I am wearing. He watches me sadly, his eyes filled with anger and heartbreak, as he scoops me up and holds me to his chest like I am precious.

"Stubborn woman, aren't you? I've been trailing you for miles, I didn't want to touch you. Not with the way you were acting like I was a stranger—image that. Can't even remember me," he jokes, looking down as he strides through the sand, making my attempt at walking pale in comparison. His eyes soften and his lips tug down. "Let go, Princess. I have you. Let go, your body needs it."

Shaking my head, I try to fight, my need to stay conscious, to know where and what is happening to me, pulling me and tying me to reality.

"Let the fuck go. You need to rest. I have you, I promise.

Nothing will hurt you while I'm here," he vows.

Maybe it's the look in his eyes, or the way he watches me, but I believe him. So I stop fighting and slide into the abyss once again.

Jarring movements wake me. My eyes flutter open. Blinking, I stare in confusion at the ground. My head is lying over an arm as I jostle in someone's hold. Turning my head seems to take a lot of effort and sends pain racking through my body, so I close my eyes again and slide back into the dark.

"Help her!" I hear the man who saved me grunt somewhere close to my head.

My eyes feel glued shut and I can't seem to open them.

"We told you, only come here in dire circumstances," an older male voice whispers in hushed tones.

"This is fucking dire. Help her and I will call us even," my savior growls, and I must whimper because he sucks in a breath, moving me in his arms. "Shh, Princess. Go back to sleep, I'm still here." His voice is so much softer and it slides through my body, warming me and comforting me.

The Forgotten

I do as I am told. It hurts too much to be awake.

Whimpering, I open my eyes and blink to clear them. My whole body feels light and I glance down at the bed I am lying on. The quilt is a patchwork of other colours and patterns obviously stitched together. My head is on a pillow of some sort and I don't feel any pain, so they must have given me some meds. Looking up, I take in the darkened room I am in. A door stands opposite me, closed and made of wood. To the right is an open window, letting in a breeze and showing me the night's sky. It's small but warm, and too dark for me to make out anything else. So when someone sits forward beside the window, breaking the shadows, I let out a yelp which turns into a hacking cough, ripping through my already sore throat.

They rush to my side and pass me some cloudy looking water. Taking a sip as I stare at where his face must be, the dark too thick to make it out.

"Thank you," I whisper as the glass is pulled away. He retreats again, only to drag the chair he was obviously sitting in closer. When he does, I can finally make out his face.

"Assassin guy?" I croak and he grins.

"The one and only, Princess, but you could just call me Archel," he jokes, leaning forward to place his elbows on his knees as he watches me.

That's when it all comes back and I close my eyes as a tear drips onto my cheek. Not only has the man seen me at my worst, but he stayed here, wherever we are, protecting me as I slept.

"Hey, none of that okay?" he says, almost begging, he sounds that pained.

Opening my eyes again with wet lashes, I stare into his. "Did they all die?" I ask, needing to know.

"Yes," he states simply, and something in me, a tension I didn't realise I was carrying, eases.

"Good," I whisper and stare back out of the window, not wanting to look at him. Shame coats my skin and I can still feel them touching me, it makes me shiver in disgust.

"Where am I?" I inquire, fighting the need to jump up and scrub at my skin until no traces of them remain.

"They are called The Forgotten. They live at the base of the mountains, away from the cannibals in what is left of the last of the vegetation. I brought you here and they patched you up. You are safe." He takes a deep breath and my eyes flicker back to him. "I didn't let any males touch you apart from me, you didn't seem to mind, and I also cleaned you myself." He holds still, like he is expecting me to flip out, but it only relieves me that I have been washed and that he did it. Although it embarasses me, I don't think I could stand the thought of some random person cleansing the evidence of my attack away, something in me trusts him.

"Thank you," I murmur and my eyes go back to the window.

I hear him sigh as he shifts in the chair. "Look, I get how you are feeling right now, okay? But you can't let this break you. You are safe here and you can rest and heal, which is what you need to do."

I ignore him and he grunts. "I mean it, you are stronger than this."

"You don't know me," I quip coldly, still feeling numb. I just want to retreat back into this darkness, and ignore the disgust and shame coursing through me. I just want to not feel again. It's easier.

"I know enough. You pulled a fucking rock out of your own leg to use as a weapon. You are a warrior through and through, you will make it," he finishes, sounding proud.

I don't respond, I just close my eyes and shift my heavy head so I am on my back.

"Sleep, I will be here when you wake up," he promises and I do.

Chapter 18
The Forgotten

I sleep on and off for the next couple of days. An older, big muscly man who Archel introduced as Simon, comes by every few hours to check my wounds. I flinched and cowered the first time he came into my room, curling in on my aching body in panic. Archel talked me through it, and refused to leave the room even when Simon glared and asked him to. Instead, he held my hand as I closed my eyes and tried to block out Simon's touch. Before leaving the first time, Simon told me to rest my voice as my throat was badly raw and inflamed. He also brought me some sweet tasting tea and told me to drink as much of it as I could.

I only looked at the devastation wrought on my body once, and it was enough for a lifetime. Bruises in various shades of purple, green, and black decorate all of my body. A bandage covers my thigh from the rock with blood soaking through it, which Simon told me off for. My thighs have teeth marks, whip marks, and worse. My back is sore and I do not bother trying to look at it. My head has a nice lump on it and the left side of it is blown up and raw looking, my eye squinting in the mess of bruises.

Despite his size, Simon is gentle. He's rough around the edges with a long, thick brown beard speckled with grey covering his chin and a matching handlebar mustache above his lip. His eyes are a deep grey and soft. He reminds me of Evvie, all hard on the outside but soft and mushy inside, not that I would say that to Simon. In fact, I don't speak at all. He speaks to me the entire time he tends to me, and I hold Archel's hand as he does so, which anchors me to the present so I can ignore the flashes of Eel's and the others' hands and mouths on me.

When he's done, he always looks at me sadly, with questions in his eyes I refuse to answer. "When you are ready, you can meet the others," he told me today. I wanted to scoff at him, I wanted to laugh and make a stupid remark...but I couldn't.

He sighed and smiled sadly before leaving. Waiting until he left the hut, I let go of Archel's hand and I curled up on my side, closing my eyes.

"You can't sleep forever," he says softly, crouching next to me. "It won't make it go away, it will still be here when you wake up."

"What would you know?" I mutter, but he obviously hears me. "More than you would think," he replies, making me freeze.

I crack open my eyes and watch as he leans back into his position next to the bed, the one he refused to leave. Closing my eyes again, I feel safe with him near. Thoughts of Evvie and Jago crowd my mind but I push them away, feeling too raw to even think about the men who hold my heart.

"You are healing well. You should be able to start moving around in a day or two. You need to go slow and have help, but it would be good to see you out of this bed," Simon informs me softly, as he wraps the bandage around my thigh. I avert my eyes, staring at the bedding.

I had faked sleep whenever anyone else had knocked at the small hut's door. Archel refused to let them in, instead he brought in their gifts for me. Some were weapons, some food, some clothing, and even a teddy bear. I refused to acknowledge them though.

"Thanks, doc," Archel grunts as Simon straightens.

He nods and looks down at me, and Simon's hand lands on my arm, making my eyes shoot to him as I freeze, panic clawing at my throat. I thought it would be worse, but I take deep breaths and concentrate on his face, on his caring, and the way he has nursed me back to health. He winces and removes the hand, looking guilty. "Sorry, just... think about it, okay?" he suggests gruffly, before turning and leaving me alone with my shadow protector.

"I need to wash," I mutter, and I feel his shock at me speaking without him having to push me.

"Okay, I'll go get the bucket—" He starts, we have done the same thing every day, or every time I start to feel their touch on my skin or think I can smell them on me.

"No, I want to wash myself. Is there a bath or a shower?" I ask, looking at the ground between us. My voice is so much better after not speaking for so long, but it still catches every now and again and breaks, but I can almost talk at a normal level now.

He's quiet for a moment before he sighs and stands up, stopping next to me. "Yes, trust me?" he inquires and I look up at him, searching his eyes. When I nod, he leans down and gently lifts me into his arms. I bury my head in his chest and let him carry me. He slips out of the door and I shake at being outside in the open, but he walks quickly and when I peek out I gape at where we are. Looking over his shoulder I can't help but notice the beauty of my surroundings.

The yellow and brown mountain towers behind us, with huts and houses dotted at the base of it and leading up the side. People bustle about, not paying attention to us. A large firepit, with a roasting section over the top, sits in the middle of camp. A dirt road leads away and between brownish looking trees. The first alive ones I have ever seen.

They aren't vibrant and green like the old pictures, more brown and greyish, but they are here. Lining between us and the rest of the world. It helps me relax for the first time since I woke up, and when Archel slides through their depths I turn my head to see where he is taking me.

Not five minutes away from camp, hiding from prying eyes, is a pond. Bigger than the gym in Paradise and filled with clearish looking water. Trees line it, shading it from the relentless sun. All I can think about is sinking into its depths and relaxing my sore and aching muscles.

"Let me down," I beg.

"You can't stand, hang on," Archel replies.

He kicks off his boots before walking into the water, clothes and all. Gripping onto his shirt I gasp when the warm water hits my body. He doesn't stop until he reaches the middle, and then he sits down with me in his arms until it reaches my chin.

Closing my eyes in bliss, I concentrate on the water as it laps against my body, carrying me away. He sits here and holds me for hours while I relax in his arms, for once not thinking.

"Are you ready to go back?" he asks, brushing my hair from my face.

"Not yet, just a bit longer?" I appeal, and he wraps his arms around me.

"Okay," he agrees.

We sit there, just relaxing until I start to get cold, then we leave the water and head back to the hut. I'm asleep again before my head hits the pillow.

The next few days are a blur. In the morning Simon comes, and after checking me over he now sits next to me and talks about anything and everything. After the first couple of days, I start to respond. After that. Archel and I head to the pond and soak for a while.

I don't even know how long it has been since my attack or what day it is, but my nights are spent in a cold sweat as nightmares cram into my head, sending me into a panic which I wake up screaming from. Archel is always there, ready to talk to me until I calm down.

During the day, my panic and shame have lessened until I can function. I still find I'm shy with new people and not wanting to be touched, but Archel and Simon seem to understand. I find my mind drifting more often than not to Jago and Evan. I miss them like crazy, and I wonder if they were told that I had died. It would make sense, the scene was carnage after all, and that's even if they venture that far into the Wastes to look for us. I know Jago will, but Paradise guards? Not so much. It pains me to learn that I turned a blind eye to the deceit and lies within the ranks and community I grew up in. I wonder if my parents knew, if that's why they left? Either way, I know I can't go back. Not after everything, and even if I saw Jago or Evan again…I'm not the same Piper. I'm not Pip and I sure as shit am not Brawler. Turning over in the bed I bury my face in the pillow as tears come again.

I didn't fight hard enough. Jago would be disgusted with me, he drilled me time and time again on what to do and I just froze. No, it's for the best if I don't go back—for them and for me.

I have a fresh start here amongst The Forgotten—because that is what I am, after all.

Chapter 19
My Shadow

I hardly know Archel, I haven't quizzed him like Jago or grown up with him like Evan. I don't even know where he comes from or where he lives out here, or how he seems to know The Forgotten and Simon, but I know the important stuff.

No matter the hard front he puts on, he cares deeply, he just doesn't let people see. He must, or why would he save me? Why would he stay by my bedside and let my tears soak his chest? Why would he spend his days holding me in water just so I can escape my own mind?

No, I don't know his past or present but I know his soul, and he will never be able to hide it from me again—but the same goes for me too. You can only cut as deep as you are willing to cut yourself. Wit, sarcasm, and jokes aside, he saw me at my darkest and at my lowest. He saw the center of me, and I will never be able to hide that from him. It creates a bond, an understanding. With one look at me, he can tell what I am feeling or if I am having a bad morning, and he just reacts. No words, they aren't needed.

"You are healing really well, you should be able to walk properly on that leg now. You are lucky it didn't tear anything. Just be careful and make sure someone is with you at all times. Take it slow," Simon finishes, sitting back on the bed after checking my injuries.

My bruising has turned that horrible shade of green and yellow, and I look like a walking wound. My face isn't as bad, the swelling started going down now, and I finally feel like I can see properly again, but it's not the damage outside that are the worst. I hate the pity party I am throwing myself, it's not like me, but I can't seem to get out of it. What was done to me was horrendous, so vile that I can barely think about it, but most of the time it feels like it happened to someone else. Simon told me yesterday that it will take me awhile to fully heal, but when I do I will be stronger and better than ever, and not to worry because if we do, wounds fester. I don't think he was talking about the ones that decorate my skin like a painting.

"How about I show you around the camp? Your shadow can come?" he offers, excitement in his eyes, and also hope. I can't bring myself to squish that again. He has been so welcoming to me, and even though I don't leave the hut except for the water, I hear his people and the laughter here. It does pique my curiosity, it's slowly coming back with each day. Simon, with his gentle hands and gruff words, has wormed his way into my heart and I would hate to stomp on his kindness, even if the thought of going outside, of being around people again, terrifies me and sends a cold shiver down my spine.

"I will be at your side, always," Archel promises, and I meet his deep blue eyes. It relaxes me and I blow out a breath before turning to Simon. I try on a smile and his eyes widen before he grins crookedly at me.

"Okay, thank you, I would like that," I reply and he beams, before it turns into a belly laugh, shaking his whole frame.

"Girl, I wondered why that fucking assassin over there was following you around like a feral and shit, but that smile tells me all I need to know. If that is how amazing you look with that fake as shit one, I bet you're a knockout with the real deal." He leans forward and whispers like Archel isn't right there, and can't hear him. "I can't wait to see the real deal, come on. Get dressed. I will wait outside."

He pats my leg and turns, leaving me with Archel. I don't even flinch at his touch anymore. I would if anyone else does and the thought makes my throat begin to close until I can't breath, but Simon pushed his way through that barrier and every time he does, I relax a little bit more. Maybe I'm not completely broken after all...just healing, like he said. What does that say about me though? Archel told me once that I was stronger than I realised, is he right? Or am I just weird? Should I still be curled up into a ball in this bed?

"What's going on?" Archel asks, crouching next to me and tilting his eyes up to mine. I don't think he even realises he does it, makes himself smaller so he won't scare me.

"Nothing," I lie, as I shuffle to the edge of the bed and swing my legs over.

"Liar, come on Princess, share," he pushes, and I roll my eyes knowing he won't drop it.

"I dunno, I just... shouldn't I be completely fucked up beyond belief ? Not laughing in here with Simon, or letting him show me around? Shouldn't I not be able to smile, shouldn't I be...broken?" I finish, looking at the floor.

He leans closer and tips my head back with a finger so I meet his eyes. "No. Everyone heals from trauma differently Princess, just because this is how you heal doesn't make it wrong or you weird. You went through hell, it makes sense you would find your own way back from that fire. It doesn't make it wrong and smiling definitely isn't a fucking sin, you should do it as often as you like and you will. You're strong, you're a fighter. This won't keep you down, and you heal however the hell you want to, don't let anyone make you feel bad about that—not even yourself. Now come on, let's get you dressed before he comes back in here and glares until you do. He's been waiting to show you around for days," Archel asserts and drops his finger from my face, leaving a burning sensation in his wake like I can still feel him there.

"I guess I never really asked where we are," I joke, but it feels strange to do so.

"Well you are about to find out, come on." He stands up and grabs my hips. I help by pushing myself up and he catches me against his chest when my weak, wobbly legs nearly give out. I breathe through it, trying to ignore the pins and needles tingling in my limbs from disuse. I guess I got used to Archel carrying me everywhere and a small part of me will miss that.

"I can dress myself," I state, and once he is sure I'm steady he steps back.

"Fine, but I'm not leaving the room. Get the fuck over it." He grins as he leans back against the wall, making me roll my eyes. I think he might even be more stubborn than me.

"Pervert," I mutter and he laughs.

"Wouldn't that be stalker?" he quips, and my lips twitch.

"True, how did you find me?" I inquire, as I reach towards the end of the bed and grab the loose fitting pants Simon brought me the other day. I can't get jeans over my legs yet, so it's just easier to wear these.

"Stalking you, of course," he teases, as I bend over and slip my good leg in the pants. I frown when I try and lift the other, the struggle is real and I feel like I'm about to fall over.

"Stubborn woman," he mutters, before striding over and sitting at my feet. I lay my hand on his shoulder as he helps lift my foot and place it in the pants. Then he drags them over my thighs and settles them on my hips.

"Seriously, how did you find me?" I repeat and he looks up, his hands still framing my hips but I've got used to him touching me.

"I was on my way back home when I saw the lights from the truck. Figured I would see what idiot had wandered too far," he explains harshly, his mouth twisting and his eyes darkening, obviously remembering how he found me.

"Thank you," I whisper, looking deep into those eyes so he can see how much I mean it.

"You're welcome Princess, now come on." He stands up and I decide to leave Archel's shirt, which I am wearing, on. I won't be winning any fashion awards, but I feel comfortable and having his scent so close is helping me.

Sighing, I grab his hand and walk towards the door of the hut.

It's slow going but my leg doesn't hurt as much as it should, and it feels good to stretch and walk again.

When I stick my head out the door I see an impatient looking Simon, so I step out into the warm midday air, with Archel, or my shadow as Simon and the others have started calling him, right behind me.

"Come on, we have missed dinner so it should be quiet as the men head out for guard duty and the others will be doing the chores for the day," he says gruffly, his hands on his hips.

I nod and step next to him, he looks down and nods in return before he starts walking. When he realises I can't keep up with his big strides, he slows right down and walks next to me, until I am framed in the middle of them both.

My hut, or what I had claimed as my hut, was apparently a new structure constructed a little higher up than some and away from most. A dirty path, with trees on either side, led down the slope to the middle of the camp then out to other huts. The hut I was staying in made me feel safe, and I was leaving that behind now and I was very aware of this.

Looking over my shoulder, I eye my new home sadly. It's not much from the outside, and inside it's just two rooms—a bedroom/living room and a bathroom. The hut is built from wood with a cut out window and a hand carved door, which is propped open, begging me to come back and hide in its depths. The mountain towers behind it, touching the sky, and it takes my breath away every time I see it. It's a beautiful place, that's for sure. The last oasis in the world, at least that's what Archel called it and he might be right.

Turning back, I make my way down the dirty path through the trees, gripping Archel to prevent myself from falling. Simon remains by my side the entire time and I decide to ask some of the questions circling in my brain.

"I know we are in the mountains and I know you are called The Forgotten, but why have I never heard of you?" I ask, keeping my eyes on the ground so I don't fall.

"Heard much about things out here, have you?" Simon coun- ters, looking down at me.

"Well, no, but I heard about the clans and I have explored— wait, out here?" I sputter, stopping and staring at him.

He grins at me. "I used to live in Paradise, in fact most people here did. That's why we are called The Forgotten. We left and never looked back, some come from other clans and we made a life here— forgotten from the rest of the world and the other clans. We just want peace." He starts walking again, forcing me to move even as shock courses through me.

"You were from Paradise and you left? My parents did the same, but apparently they died," I inform him sadly. I can feel Archel watching me, no doubt storing everything he is learning about me away.

"I am sorry about that Piper, not everyone makes it. Ferals, clans, and raiders pick off anyone they can find." He eyes me sadly. "Not to mention Paradise Captains and guards themselves," he adds.

"What do you mean?" I ask, trying to catch his eye.

He blows out a breath and turns, stopping and blocking my path. "Look kid, I know it was Paradise guards who attacked you, Shadow here told me. You think you are the only one? They don't like people leaving and they make sure they stop it if they can— even killing people if they have to. Women? They attack them and kill them. If they can't have us, no one can. Some of us managed to slip by, using friends or skills we learned, but others weren't so lucky. That's why there are a lot more men here than women, they don't let them go. Ever." He eyes me and I swallow hard.

"I didn't know," I whisper.

"Of course you didn't. Most people in Paradise don't. It starts at the top, but only a select few are part of their kill squad. The rest are just as innocent as you and I. They hide a lot down in that bunker."

I search his face for answers. "So, why did you leave?"

He grunts, the sound so similar to Jago that I stumble back into Archel.

"I was one of the doctors down there, they started asking me to go on patrols and supply missions. I was young and stupid so I agreed. I wanted to know what it was like out here. The missions...they showed me the truth of the guards and people. Greed, and the things they did. I couldn't stand by and watch that happen, I was a doctor for fuck's sake. I promised to do no harm, and they made me. I couldn't do that. So, I got a few like-minded people and on the next mission we volunteered to check out a build- ing, and we escaped and never looked back. We stumbled across the Wastes for a while before we found this place—and the people already here. People just wanting peace, it seemed right so we stayed."

We start walking again and the smell of roasting meat and fire reaches me as I hear voices. It sends a spike of panic through me but I force it down. "You are the leader of The Forgotten?" I ques- tion instead, concentrating on speaking.

He laughs, throwing his head back, sending crows perched on the trees flying. "Sands, no. That would be Trev. He came to see you while you were out of it, he would be happy to meet you. I'm just the medic here."

We break through the trees and my jaw drops. I guess every time we came near here I buried my head, not wanting to see anyone, but I don't how I ignored all of this. This isn't a camp—it's a community. A town set at the base of the mountains. An oasis surviving the end of the world.

Huts of all sizes surround a cleared section of ground, the trees lining the clearing and blocking us from the rest of the world. A massive firepit sits in the middle with something roasting above it. Logs fashioned into benches a circle around it, and just before the trees are some mismatched tables and chairs. Each hut is a different colour and made from different materials, but mainly wood and what looks like metal and stone.

We carry on walking, and Simon smiles and nods at a few women and men milling about the fire. They smile and wave, even at me, and I find myself smiling back.

We walk around the clearing and onto a small dirt road, with huts lining each side like the old-school streets you saw before the end. One even has a mailbox with what looks like hand painted flowers on it.

At the end of the road and sitting on a hill leading up to the mountain, is what looks like a huge tent. White and imposing, and covered here and there with sand obviously from the wind, it stands like a beacon to the rest of the community. Two large firepits are placed on either side of an open entrance, guiding the way even when not lit.

"What is that?" I ask as I start to slow, tired from only walking this far. Archel, obviously noticing, wraps his arm around my waist and keeps us moving.

"We call it City Hall, but it's where we hold our meeting, sometimes where we meet, where we celebrate...it's our center. Where our community gathers," Simon answers. "As our tribe gets bigger, the more we need it."

"You keep getting bigger?" I press for information, leaning more heavily on Archel, not that he seems to mind.

"Yup, your shadow there sometimes directs people he trusts here or people find us by themselves."

I look up at Archel with an arched eyebrow and he winks at my expression. "I don't do it for them, Princess, so don't think I'm some kind of hero. It just keeps them in my debt."

"Sure thing Shadow, you tell yourself that," I tease.

"Don't let him fool you girl, he keeps our secret and not just because he likes being a know it all," Simon adds.

"So why do you do it?" I address Archel.

He shrugs, watching the huts as we pass. "They want to live in peace. I might not believe that it can happen in this world, but it doesn't mean I should throw them to wolves out there. Plus, it's a nice place to get some down time when I need it."

I can't help the grin that splits my face. "You're such a softie," I whisper loudly.

He rolls his eyes. "Not really, Princess. Keep poking and I'll show you how not soft I am."

I choke on a laugh before it tumbles free. I can't help it, I laugh until tears stream down my face. Everything bursting out in the desperate, hysterical sound.

They both stop and stare at me in awe. "Told you." Simon grins at me before turning back to the tent as my chuckles finally die off.

We walk in silence the rest of the way, letting me take in the views. When we reach the tent a smaller man steps out. When he spots us, he grins. Simon nods and makes his way over and embraces the man. Archel drags me closer and I wait as Simon steps to the man's side to introduce us.

"Piper, meet Trev. Trev, meet our latest survivor." My eyes widen and I swing them back to the smaller man.

This man runs this place? He's skinny, really skinny, but the type that you can tell is just naturally like that. He's older than me and even Simon, probably in his sixties. Long grey and silver hair hangs over his shoulder in a braid, with feathers and beads threaded throughout. His skin is tanned and wrinkled, and his face is kind and open with big brown eyes and small thin lips. He's clean-shaven though and his clothes are loose fitting, like he doesn't care what he looks like. It's so opposite of the leaders of Paradise that I do a double take.

His eyes dance with amusement but he doesn't extend his hand, I'm guessing Simon warned him. "Nice to meet you Piper. I saw you when you first came in." My back stiffens but he carries on, "You are one hell of a fighter, I'm glad you could come here. Archel, nice to see you as always." He greets the man at my side, and to my shock, Archel smiles and lowers his head in submission.

"Trev, good to see you old man," he jokes and I elbow his side, which only makes them all laugh.

"Don't fret, Piper. He's always been like this, even when he was younger. I am used to it. Come in, let's get you sitting down, and I'm sure you have questions." He waves us inside and I hesitate. "Your shadow can come too, I have heard you don't go anywhere without him."

"Thank you, and thank you for letting me stay. You didn't have to," I reply kindly as I start past him, Archel by my side and Simon at my back.

"Of course I did, all lost souls are welcome here with The Forgotten," he responds as the tent door closes behind us, and once again my jaw drops at the view before me. They continue to surprise me and the Hall is no different than the rest of the community. They might be forgotten, but they sure as hell haven't disappeared.

Chapter 20
Questions

The tent, which I guess you can't really call a tent considering the inside looks like something out of a magazine mixed with a medieval castle, is amazing. Rugs in all different colours lay across the larger space. Crossed swords stand at the very back, above a wooden chair with carved arms. More chairs are scattered through- out. As is what looks like a bar to the right with homemade brews and liquor. To the left are cushions lying everywhere for people to relax.

"Take a seat, let's talk," Trev says and strides past us. I figured he would pick the big chair in the center, but he chooses one at random and sits down. Simon grabs three others and makes a circle with him included.

Archel helps me sit in one before grabbing another and spinning it, straddling the seat and resting his chin on the back of it.

"So, Piper. You are from Paradise, correct?" Trev asks and I nod.

"Yes, sir," I reply automatically.

"No sir here, just Trev." He grins, his eyes dancing. "I heard of your attack, please take all the time you need to heal and know we are here for you when you need it. I would also like to have a chat with you tomorrow if we could? I shall bring some tea and we can discuss things further?" He offers, watching me kindly.

"Sounds good," I agree and he smiles wide.

"Brilliant! Now, I can almost hear the questions turning around in your brain. Fire away."

"How are you left alone out here? From other clans and such?" I start and he nods, his face turning thoughtful.

"Honestly, luck. None of them know we are here. The clans don't venture this way for fear of the cannibals that live below the mountain, and the ferals that live on the other side. We have had the odd one or two wander in, but nothing we couldn't take care of."

"Simon said you are all from clans or Paradise, where are you from?"

He smiles at me again. "I was part of a clan called the Seekers, the very one your shadow is from. Have you heard of it?"

I look over at Archel in shock, but he just stares blankly back at me. "Jag- I mean my friend told me bits," I admit.

"Ah, probably all bad?"

I nod and he shakes his head sadly. "It wasn't all bad, but the old leader went off his rails a bit. When he killed my Sarah, my wife, I left. It wasn't until I saw Archel years later that he informed me the leadership had changed."

"I'm sorry," I reply honestly. "Changed to who?"

"I think your shadow could answer your question better," he redirects and I turn my attention to Archel.

Tilting his head to face me, he presses his cheek to the top of the chair. "Dray, my brother in arms. He's a good man."

I ponder that—a good man? Jago didn't describe it this way, but I guess if he came to Paradise at thirteen then he has been out of the loop for a while. "You are part of the Seekers?" I ask, shifting nervously.

"I am, I'm his right-hand man. His assassin," he discloses freely, holding my eyes without shame. I knew what he was though, he must have forgotten I saw him fight that day.

"Okay." I turn back Trev to see him watching the interaction with a small, strange smile. "I'm sure I have more, but honestly I can't seem to remember," I admit, a bit embarrassed.

"Not to worry, join me for tea tomorrow and you can ask then." He stands and I struggle to my feet. "For now, I must see to the rounds." He nods at us all before striding away, faster than I thought possible for such an older man. "Tomorrow," he reminds me, before ducking out of the tent and leaving me with Archel and Simon.

"You should rest now, this will have taken a lot out of you," Simon orders and leaves as well.

"Come on," Archel says, but I am determined to walk so I squeal when he lifts me into his arms, holding me effortlessly against his chest.

"What the hell, dude?" I yelp.

"You heard him, you need to rest." He grins, looking down at me.

"I could have walked," I protest and he rolls his eyes.

"Maybe I wanted to carry you," he murmurs and that shuts me up.

Snuggling against his chest I let his movements comfort me, and before I know it my eyes are sliding shut.

I woke the next morning, still in Archel's shirt and fully rested, and feeling itchy. I want to move, now that I've been out I don't want to be cramped up in here.

"Can we go to the water?" I ask, my eyes seeking out Archel who I know will be watching somewhere close by.

"Whatever you wish, Princess." He flourishes a bow and steps forward.

I slide from the bed before he can carry me and he grabs my arm. "No point putting on your trousers, they will only get wet. Come on." He leads me out the door and I follow.

When we get to the water he holds my arm as I wade through to the middle, and when I sit down he sits behind me, pulling me back to his chest as his legs spread on either side of mine.

We sit in silence for a while, just watching the world until I break the stillness. "I know how to fight, I was in training before...but you know how to. I've seen it. You move faster than I can blink and no one manages to land a hit. Will you teach me?"

I feel him suck in a breath. "You want me to teach you to be an assassin?"

"No, I want you to teach me to never be weak again. I want you to teach me to be a true warrior," I clarify, swishing my fingers through the water next to us.

"Are you sure?" he inquires, his breath stirring my hair.

"Yes, I think it will help. I know the basics, but I didn't have time to learn much more," I admit and it sends a throb through my heart, along with a sense of deja vu of me asking Jago to train me. I wonder if he has stopped searching yet? It would be for the best. He might not love the Wastes, but he doesn't belong out here—not again. No, he was happy in Paradise before I came along, and he will be happy again.

"Okay, Princess," Archel whispers, before dropping his chin on my shoulder.

A true, real smile covers my face and I feel something in me click back into place. I might not be healed, I might not be okay anytime soon, but for the first time since the attack I start to feel more like myself, like I am taking charge of my life again and I have my shadow to thank for that.

Who knew such tragedy could lead to such belonging?

Chapter 21
Game On

"How come your trees aren't dead?" I ask curiously. Trev came by the hut just after I had finished dressing, and he escorted me back down to the clearing where he had set up a blanket and some pillows with a log to lean on. Archel followed us, he didn't think I noticed but I saw him dash into the trees, and my eyes were drawn to the shadows where he is currently watching us from. What a stalker, the thought makes me grin.

Trev has been answering my questions for the last hour or so, but I am content to just enjoy his company and I think he feels the same way. Something about him soothes me, he reminds me of my dad in a comforting way.

"They are getting there, we are trying to save them even as the Wastes tries to reclaim them," Trev answers, reclining back next to me. For someone in charge of a whole settlement, or tribe as they call it, he sure is relaxed. Just being with him sets me at ease, like with Simon. Odd that I would find that with strange males, but whatever works.

"Will you go back?" he questions suddenly, and I mull over his questions.

"No. That is my past, plus they would kill me. I just wish I could speak to my friends, to let them know I'm okay."

"Are you?" he presses, turning to look me in the eyes, his are all seeing and filled with knowledge beyond my years.

"I will be," I promise as I look back at the trees.

"I do not doubt it. Stay, stay here with us. See if you like it, we could always do with more able bodies and you love the land like we do. I see it in your eyes."

"You'd let me stay?" I ask quietly. It's what I want more than anything, at least for now.

"Yes Piper, I see something in you, something you yourself don't see," he explains, turning to me once again.

"What's that?" I inquire curiously.

"Your future. You are destined for great things, and I hope that includes you being here with us," he finishes, and he sighs as he stands. "I better get back. Lots to do." He starts to walk away and I bite my lip before standing as well, I see Archel break away from the shadows in the trees where he was hiding.

"Thank you, Trev. For giving me a chance, I won't let you down," I vow.

"I know you won't, when you are ready for that greatness, come and see me again. Until then, I enjoyed our little chat, maybe we could make it a daily thing?" he suggests and I nod eagerly. He smiles before turning and wandering away as Archel steps in front of me.

"You wanted me to train you?" he challenges and I groan, leaning my head back. Why do I get myself into these situations? I am betting Archel doesn't give orgasms for rewards like Jago. Bloody men. He grins wickedly, making me narrow my eyes.

"We will go easy at first, you are still recovering, but then all bets are off." He grabs my hand and starts to pull me away from mine and Trev's little nest, which I eye sadly. Me and my stupid bright ideas, I just know he is going to kick my ass and not in a good way. I wonder if I can distract him with boobs? Probably not, he will just laugh and carry on. Crazy bastard.

Huffing, I lie on the ground and curse the crazy bastard standing over me, grinning. They are creative insults as well, I need to remember them to use later on.

"Get up, Princess," he mocks and steps back.

He is taking a sick sort of enjoyment out of this. I bet it's payback for me smacking him in my sleep last night. Fuck nugget— oooh another one. Groaning, I roll to my feet. My thigh protests with a small twinge but I ignore it. The Wastes are not going to wait for me to heal, and who knows how long Archel will be here? He doesn't seem like the type to stick around, so I need to get the most out of him while I can.

He watches me as I run through the moves he taught me with the knife. I almost screamed in happiness when he gave it to me. He didn't seem to have any worries about starting with hand-to-hand, and when I asked him he got all serious and told me that out here, my opponents and attackers aren't going to wait for me to punch them, and using weapons will give me an advantage. I didn't ask any more questions after that and it feels nasty to even admit, but he's right. Not that I will tell him that, his head would get too big and he would probably float into the sky like a fucking balloon.

"Good, now let's see which weapons you are best with," he orders, sliding over to me and opening a bag I didn't notice before.

"Huh?" I ask dumbly.

"I need to see which ones you have natural talent with, we don't have a lot of time so it makes sense for us to narrow your skill set just to what you can use for now. Later we can add more," he mutters, as he flings weapons out on the ground next to the bag. My eyes widen with each one, there is everything you could imagine in there and it makes me a tiny bit worried that he carries this around with him, but it also makes me feel safe.

A mace, sword, whip, knives, throwing stars, crossbow, katanas, chains, bow, guns, and others which I don't even know what the hell they are.

"Er... overkill much?" I joke, and he looks up at me from his crouched position next to the bag.

"You never know out there, plus I like to collect." He winks.

"You collect weapons?" I question, astonished, but of course he does.

"Yup, you've got to have hobbies." He laughs as he adds more to the growing pile.

Hobbies. That makes me think of fucking knitting or some shit, not collecting an armory and toting it around with you like a unicorn backpack. Just when I think I have him all figured out, he does some crazy shit like this.

"Okay, I think that is all," he mutters seriously, digging through the bag.

"Sure, didn't bring your machine gun?" I tease, propping my hands on my hips. It feels weird to be joking and laughing, like I shouldn't, but Archel throws me a look and that feeling disappears. His eyes laugh at me, filled with naughty things that I shouldn't be looking too closely at, not after what happened.

"Nah, I left that behind. I'll bring it next time, might be too big for you though." He stands and claps his hands as I gawk at him.

"You have a machine gun?" I drawl slowly, blinking at him.

He winks as a grin tugs at his full lips, and I am struck once again by how beautiful he is. I guess I was ignoring that while I was healing, but now that I am reminded of it, it's all I can see.. "Sure, I have another machine gun right here if you want to see?" he quips, cupping himself, but then he freezes and stares at me as if remembering why he shouldn't joke like that. It makes me roll my eyes at his concern, because I'm not a broken fucking thing like he said, and I never want him to censor himself around me.

"Sure you do. I bet it's more like a little knife," I taunt and his grin turns wicked.

"Even little things like that could do some damage, want to see?"

He moves closer, the weapons in a pile at our feet and I doubt they are what we are even talking about anymore, but that doesn't bother me. I know this is just flirting and it makes me feel good that he still sees me that way.

"I'd rather play with a sword." I grin and he laughs, stepping back.

"Woman after my own heart, come on then Princess. Pick your first weapon and let's see what fire you got in that sexy body of yours." He picks up the bag and walks over to the edge of the clearing, leaving me staring after him once again. He thinks I'm sexy? It sends a bolt of lust through me, which soon turns to confusion. *Fuck, I am so messed up.*

Ignoring the mess that is my head and emotions, I lean down and grab a huge two handed sword. I nearly drop it, my arms already shaking from the weight. "That won't work," he comments, circling me, and I go to snark back but I see the seriousness and concentration on his face. He really is trying to help. So for once I hold back my sass and drop the big metal sword to the pile with a clank. Thinking seriously this time, I eye the pile for something I think I could work with.

"You're small with shorter arms, it would be good to have something you could use first before they got too close to inflict some damage. Maybe a distance weapon and a close contact one would be good to train you in first," he suggests and I nod. It makes me wonder about him though. Trev called him an assassin and I saw him fight that day with Jago. He's the Seeker's assassin, does he just hunt around the Wastes all the time? That must get lonely.

Bending down I sift through the weapons, trying not to hurt myself, but with a yelp I hold my finger up to see blood welling at the tip from where I caught it on something sharp. Archel is there in a instant. Crouched in front of me, his fingers cupping mine. He eyes the weapons like they have betrayed him before pulling my injured finger closer. My chest rattles and my breathing seems to stop as he pulls it to his mouth and sucks the blood away. My pussy throbs in time with my heartbeat, and my breathing picks up as my heart hammers so loud he must hear it. With his eyes locked on mine with a scary intensity, his crazy swirling in their oceanic depths, he slowly pulls my finger from his mouth and I swallow hard, forcing myself to look down.

The blood is gone and there is only a tiny cut, so I tug it from his grasp and hold it protectively to my chest. "Thanks," I mutter, my voice breathless.

"Be careful, I can't kill them," he replies before standing up and stepping back, leaving me confused. Did he mean he can't kill the weapons for hurting me? Here I thought Jago was crazy and over-protective, but Archel was just down right mental. He's smooth and pops up like the dark, whereas Jago is brutal and unforgiving, barging his way into the light. Archel doesn't want that, he likes the dark and pain and bloodshed but he can be rough when he needs to. Shaking my head, I try to stop comparing them. Instead, I eye the weapons again. He said long distance. Nibbling on my lower lip, I carefully reach down and extract three throwing stars that make me feel like a ninja.

"Good choice. Okay, let's see how accurately you can throw," he orders, and I nod as I get to my feet, carefully holding them so I don't cut myself again.

I follow him over to a tree where he stops me with a hand on my hip, before he walks over and nails a target into the bark. When he's happy, he walks back over and stands next to me.

"Okay, let me show you first." He grabs one from me and without even looking, throws it at the tree where it buries into the bullseye. That's freaking impressive and a little bit hot. "Your turn." He steps behind me and guides me into the correct position, and then steps back again.

Taking a deep breath I push the feel of him behind me away, and concentrate on the bullseye. Determination races through me as I pull my hand back and let it loose. It hits the target and bounces off onto the ground, making me wince. Okay, so maybe not so ninja-like.

"Maybe not throwing stars." Archel laughs and I spin with

narrowed eyes. He holds his hands up and I cross mine, as he walks back over to the pile of weapons and starts looking through them. Grabbing something, he makes his way back over to me and presents it.

"A crossbow?" I ask, incredulously.

"Yes. It's harder to master, but longer distance and easier to aim." He turns me around and places it in my arms, a bolt already loaded.

"Okay, so this one has a crosshair sight, make sure to keep your hands on the rail below so they don't get anywhere near the string. I'll show you how to cock it and reload after, but for now I want you to bring it up to your shoulder." He steps back as I test the weight. It's heavy but not so heavy that I can't hold it.

Resting the butt on my shoulder, I peer through the scope with one eye.

"Click off your safety." He shows me how and I do so before looking back in the scope. "If shooting normally, you will need to think about wind and so forth, but let's not worry about that today. I want you to squeeze the trigger once you have it lined up," he says calmly, his voice soothing and reassuring.

Breathing out, I squeeze the trigger as the bolt releases from the bow and flies through the air. Dropping it, so it points at the ground I gawk at the target where the bolt sticks dead center.

"You're a natural." Archel grins, pride filling his eyes, and I can't help but smile in return.

"Can you show me how to reload?" I request giddily, loving the feel of the weapon in my hands.

He nods and puts the safety on as he demonstrates how to load the bow. I run through it a few times and once he is happy, he lets me play. I manage to hit dead center every time, and each bolt only adds to my confidence, something I haven't felt since the attack.

"I'll make sure to bring you a loader and a new bow back," he comments idly as he watches me, making sure I don't hurt myself. Dropping the bow to point at the ground I look at him in confusion.

"Back from where?" I inquire, frowning hard.

"I need to head out soon, check on a few things, but I'll be back," he adds when he sees my face drop. I school it and nod and go back to shooting, with a sour taste in my mouth at the thought of being without him. I guess I have got used to him always being here, like a security blanket.

"Okay, how about we practise more with this later? Let's find you a close range weapon," he murmurs, as he heads back over to the pile.

I lose one more arrow before putting on the safety and lying it softly down next to me. Staring at the arrows I wrap my arms around my middle, shivering despite the heat. I guess I knew he would leave at some point, I just wish it wasn't yet.

"Princess," he shouts, and when I blink I find him in front of me. From the way he is speaking, it's clear he has said my name a few times before.

"Huh?" I ask dumbly.

"I'll be back, I promise you," he declares softly.

I scoff and try to cover my emotions, he already sees too much. "Don't get cocky, I just zoned out is all."

He cocks his eyebrow at me and just stares until I start to fidget, uncomfortable with the way he is watching me, like he sees everything I am trying to hide.

"Are we training or what?" I ask quickly and his lips twitch.

Leaning forward so our mouths are inches apart he stops and I freeze, fear and excitement war inside me as I try to figure out how I am feeling. "You don't get rid of me that easily, Princess. You owe me a debt, a life for a life and I plan on taking yours. I won't kill you, don't worry. No, you are much more interesting alive. Your life is mine, you are mine." He leans back and turns around casually, like nothing just happened, as I gawk at him.

"I noticed you eyeing the katana. Now, it's nothing fancy and I'm not an expert, I am better with knives, swords, and guns, but I can teach you some. It's smaller so should be better for you grip." He carries on while I just stare at him, wondering what the hell just happened.

Did the assassin just...claim me? Like some old-school mating bullshit? He has another thing coming if he thinks this is how it's going to go down. I might not have been my usual sassy, fiery self, but if he keeps on pushing like that then he will realise under the fear and pain is rock-solid concrete.

Nobody, no matter how fucking pretty they are, decides anything for me. Maybe it's time I showed my shadow that.

With fresh determination and fire running through my body, I commit to becoming the old Piper... just more improved and with more scars.

Game on, Shadow.

Chapter 22
Baby Steps

Archel spends hours training me, mainly on how to handle the sword and a few basic movements, but my body isn't one hundred percent yet and I tire quickly. When he noticed my arm dropping for the hundredth time, he calls it a day and ignores my protests, claiming he can smell food cooking anyway and that he needs sustenance to maintain all his 'amazing muscles.'

I might have scoffed at that, even as my eyes dropped to his well-defined chest and arms, and obviously he caught me if his smirk is anything to go by.

"I'm going to wash up," I declare, leaving him to pack up as I venture the couple hundred feet to the pond. With each step my heart rate increases and my breathing turns shallow, my eyes dart everywhere to check my surroundings, and I jump at every little noise. By the time I make it to the water, I am tightly strung. Determined to do this alone, I wade in and keep my eyes on the shore, washing quickly.

When I'm done, I make my way out and head back to Archel. I find him in the exact same position, but nothing seems to be packed away. I eye him strangely, but triumph rocks through me at being able to go by myself. Baby steps, and before I know it I will be back to my normal, sarcastic self.

"You ready to head for food?" I ask, starting to help him gather everything up. My anxiety bleeds away with him by my side again and my thigh takes that moment to twinge, reminding me I'm pushing myself.

"Come on, Princess. That leg of yours must be hurting by now." He heaves the bag over his shoulder and grabs my hand. We walk slowly towards the center of the settlement where I can already here the hustle and bustle. It makes my shoulders tense, but I breathe through it and hold on tighter to Archel.

"You're not half bad with a bow," he praises, obviously trying to break the tension he can feel in me.

Rolling my eyes I follow him as the sun starts to set, throwing red and orange across the sky. The fire is roaring and something is cooking, smelling delicious. I don't have the balls to ask what it is, it's not like you see any cows or pigs about nowadays.

The residents of the settlement are all here. With the tables full of people who are laughing and talking and eating. Nearly all the logs are full as well, and people are spread out on the ground, happy just to be together. It's so different from the clinical eating space at Paradise that I just stop and stare. Archel stops with me and looks from me to them. "I wish my parents were alive, they would have loved this," I whisper, my voice choked.

He looks back over at the center and seems to see it in new light. "I love it here, it's so peaceful when the rest of my life is filled with bloodshed and fighting."

He pulls me along after him before I can ask more questions about his life. We end up queuing and receiving plates filled with charred meat. Instead of leading me to a table or a log, he pulls me over to some cushions far enough away from everyone so I can relax. We sit side by side and eat as we watch everyone. Once I've finished I lean back and watch Trev as he moves through the crowd, they love him and it's more like a family than anything else.

"What about your family?" I question, breaking the silence.

I look over as he stretches out next to me, his arms behind his head as he looks up at the stars.

"Never knew them," he mutters.

Laying down next to him, I curl into his side for warmth and he turns his head to face me, the fire dancing across his cheeks. "What do you mean?"

"Dray's father was our leader when I was a kid. A year after I was born, my mother and father tried to leave to protect me. He killed them because of it and I was tossed to the other Seekers to be brought up." He says it so matter-of-factly, like it doesn't matter, but I see the slight tightening of his eyes.

"That must have been rough," I reply softly.

He shrugs and looks back at the sky. "I learned a lot of skills, like how to be a thief, how to fight, how to protect myself. Then I met Dray and the rest is history."

I nod, my eyes stuck on his face. He really is beautiful, in a deadly way. "So you just roam about the Wastes killing people?" I ask, curious.

"That bother you, Princess?" he teases, his lips quirked up.

"Not really, just more curious than anything," I admit and he turns to look at me, obviously checking if I'm being serious.

"I don't always kill people, sometimes I am sent to find people or learn things. I would do anything for Dray, for our people. They are my family."

I sigh and look down at the ground. "I can understand that."

He moves, wrapping his arm around me when I shiver, and pulls me closer to his side. "The boyfriend? That big, mean looking bastard?"

I laugh, shaking my head. "That's Jago. I had- have- had a best friend back at Paradise. We grew up together. I would have done anything for him," I divulge sadly.

"But not anymore?" he presses, knowing I am not telling him everything. He always sees too much.

"Maybe not, he hurt me. I'm betting he isn't even looking for me," I mutter and he sighs again.

"That's probably for the best, Princess. Life out here isn't made for everyone, and if he starts asking too many questions they will kill him."

I suck in a breath and let it out shakily, knowing he is right.

Looking up, I rove my eyes over his face. "You said you understood, about my attack?"

He grins, but it's not a nice one at all. "Caught that, did you?

You sure don't pull your punches..."

It's my turn to smirk at him. "No, I say what I want. It's better to be told no than to never ask."

He shakes his head and looks back at the sky. "Let's just say no one cares what happens to an orphaned street kid."

My heart breaks a little, imagining a small Archel trying to fight for his life and suffering through the unspeakable. "I dunno, you didn't turn out too bad," I joke and he laughs, his body shaking next to me.

"Knew you liked me, Princess. Just a matter of time before you love me," he taunts.

I groan and try to roll away, but he keeps me there. "Insufferable prick is what you are."

"You love it," he mocks, and I try to keep my smile in because he's right, I do.

Chapter 23

Fuck, Kill, Eat

"**G**et up!" Groaning, I burrow my head in the pillow. Why are all the men I meet such early risers? Can't we just train after dinner? "Come on, Princess. We are training with your bow before your daily meeting with Trev, then your sword after."

Rolling onto my back, I slit open my eyes to see an already dressed and put together Archel. "I hate you," I moan as I sit up and push back my tangled locks.

"No you don't, get up." He claps again and I stumble to my feet, wincing when my leg protests. He's there instantly, catching me with a worried look in his eyes.

"Fine, I'm fine. I just moved too fast," I mutter groggily.

"Didn't help that you were tossing and turning and screaming all night," he replies and I look away ashamed, but he brings my chin up. "Nothing to be embarrassed about Princess, I have night- mares too. Why do you think I hardly sleep? Next time you wake up in a cold sweat, I'll be there." Then he steps back and turns away, leaving me to get dressed. Crazy bastard. I get dressed without his help today and it makes me feel better. Right until we head outside and he walks me to our little training ground. I think he might be more of a slave driver than Jago.

Two hours later, I'm sweating my tits off. I thought training in the gym was bad, doing it under the intense heat that doesn't give up with a crazy assassin continually shouting 'again' tops that. But while I was training, I wasn't thinking, and it helps my mind become clearer and less muddled.

We break for my meeting with Trev. Archel drops me off at the cushions in the clearing, which have already been set up, and tells me he will be close by. When I search for him, I spot him sitting on a branch of a tree nearby.

Trev turns up not five minutes later, two cups of tea in his hands as he sits slowly down on the cushion next to me, but he can't fool me anymore. I've seen how fast he can move, he makes himself look weaker than he is, I wonder why.

"Good training?" he asks, passing me the tea.

Instead of staring into the woods today, I turn and sit cross-legged, holding the warm mug in my sweaty hands as I face him. His lips quirk but he copies the movements.

"I'm getting better..." I trail off as he sips his tea.

"You have something to ask, please do," he prods and I nod. "You asked me to stay, you said I belonged here. Maybe you are right, maybe you're not, but I wanted to know what you want from me if I choose to stay, and can I leave at any point?" I get my questions out and when I've finished he sips his tea, debating his answers.

"It is true, I would like you to stay, but the truth is everyone's free to leave whenever they want. They just don't, not when you have seen what is left out there. As for what I want from you, I want your mind and your trust."

I grip the mug tighter. "What does that even mean?"

"It means warrior, I see the intellect shining in your eyes. The way you see things and the world, and I have no doubt you will be even able to keep up with your shadow soon. I could do with someone like that by my side." He must see the panic on my face because he laughs. "I don't mean leading. I mean as council, someone to lean on. It's been a long time since I have been out there, same for most others here, but you have and you know Paradise."

I mull over his words as I sip the herbal tasting tea. "It has nothing to do with the fact I seem to have the assassin's loyalty?" I ask, making him laugh.

"It was a factor of course, I am not stupid Piper. He is a good weapon to have on our side."

I grit my teeth and look away, right at Archel. "He is more than just a weapon," I defend, and when I look back I see Trev grinning.

"Good, the fact you see him as more only proves my point. I need someone to be here, to call me on my bullshit. I need new blood, or I fear The Forgotten may be more than just a name."

Sipping my tea, I think over his words so I don't jump to a decision. "Well, it's not like I have anywhere else to go," I joke and he smiles softly at me.

"There is always a choice Piper, but life is too short for second guessing and worrying. It can disappear in the blink of an eye, from one moment to the next, you could just be gone. I've experienced enough loss in my life to know that lesson well, our world isn't made for the soft, so you have to create it yourself. Live every moment like it's your last, because it very well might be."

Eyeing the brownish liquid in my cup, I smile at his words. "I would like to stay, for now, if you will have me. You can teach me about your people, our land and this world, and I will help where I can. Deal?" I offer, holding out my hand.

He ignores it and leans forward, embracing me. I stiffen at first but soon relax. "Family doesn't shake hands, and Piper, you are family now."

I lean back and he lets me go. "Your shadow wants you, come to me tomorrow after training and your check up with Simon, and I will start my teachings." He stands slowly, cracking his back as he holds his hand out for my mug. I quickly down the lukewarm tea and he wanders away. I watch him go. He's a strange one for sure, but he's lived a thousand lives and pains, that much is obvious. The idea of a family again, it's appealing. I just hope it's not all lies, but I will be ready incase it is.

Archel plops down opposite me and I lean back into the pillows. "Back to training?" I guess.

He shakes his head. "Nope, I have to leave tomorrow so I figured we could have the afternoon off and just relax and enjoy it here."

"You're leaving tomorrow?" I echo, disappointment lacing my voice.

He leans forward, catching my eyes. "I will be back in five days. In those five days, I want you to practice because I will test you when I get back. If you do well enough, I will give you a present. Five days, Princess. That's all you get away from me. Try not to get into too much trouble." He waggles his eyebrows, making me laugh. "Fine, so what do you want to do?" I question, smiling as the sun bears down on me.

He winks and I roll my eyes. "How about I show you why I love this place, besides the free food and trees."

He shows me around Paradise, showing me the mountains, the land, the food, and the people, and when the sun starts to set he leads me back to the middle again.

I thought he would take me away from the crowd and show me something, but instead he seems to know something I don't, because he grabs my hand and leads me towards the Hall. When inside, he slips to the back as people start streaming in. I watch in interest and then suddenly music splits the air. My eyes round, and I zone in on the record player in the corner, the music flowing from it as people pour drinks and start to dance. All the furniture has been moved from the middle of the room, and now it's a dance floor. I even see Trev busting some moves.

I can't help the smile crossing my face, lighting it up. This place is more of a paradise than that bunker ever was, if only there were two annoying men here with me. Instead I will have to settle for the one by my side.

"Dance with me," I demand, and he looks down at me with an arched eyebrow.

"I don't dance," he grumbles, looking back at the moving bodies.

"Why? Not enough places to hide?" I joke, as I step backward, my hand held out to him. I've had enough hiding in the corners and shadows, no doubt I will retreat every now and again when I feel too raw, but right now I want to dance and have fun, with Archel.

He narrows his eyes at me, almost blending with the shadows back here. I know he has had a bad life, and he prefers the dark to the light, he makes every attempt to know what is going to happen and plans for the worst, but I don't think he's ever actually stopped and enjoyed the present. I wonder how many times he has watched from the shadows as the people here celebrate, live their lives, and dance and laugh? Does he wish he could? That's the thing about life, you could hide in the dark and death, but it won't matter in the end, it doesn't matter how much you laughed, loved, or hurt—in the end it's all about living in the moment, even if later on you regret it.

"Dance with me, Archel?" I whisper.

The room fades away as he stares at me, his eyes wide and darting to the dancing then back to me with nerves. Give this man a battle and he is fine, but faced with one woman and some music, he turns into a lost little boy. I guess we are all more damaged than I thought, but that's the thing about damaged people, together they can be whole.

He swallows hard, his Adam's apple bobbing with the movement before placing his hand in mine. I know the importance of this moment, and I squeeze his hand in thanks for him trusting me.

Turning, I pull him behind me. I don't head straight to the center of the dancing. I don't want to put on a show, that's not what this is about. Instead I pull him to the edge and spin to face him. People are swaying along, others are slow dancing, some are head- banging. Anything goes.

Archel surprises me by pulling me into his arms. Pressed against his chest, I tilt my head up to see his face. His eyes scan the people and everything, and they are tense, even his arms and body are like steel. I don't think he even knows how to turn off.

"Play a game with me." I grin and he looks down at me in confusion.

"What, like fireball?" His eyes are so confused that a startled laugh slips out.

"Fireball? What the hell, crazy pants? I was thinking like I fucking Spy, not let's burn down the entire village." Giggling, I grip his shirt as he smiles down at me, dimples appearing in his cheeks that I never knew he had and holy koala shit, why the hell are dimples like kryptonite? I swear, he could even put it in my ass and I wouldn't care as long as he kept flashing those cute motherfucking hypnotizers.

"Piper," he says, exasperated, and I frown when said dimples disappear.

"Hmm?" I ask, reaching up and pulling his lips up to try and catch them again.

"What the fuck are you doing?" he inquires, but it comes out muffled, seeing as I am playing Picasso with his face.

"Trying to make those little dips of happiness and orgasms appear," I murmur in concentration, and he freezes up and stops swaying, and when I catch his eyes he stares at me before bursting into laughter. His whole face turns red and I drop my hands as he laughs so hard people look over in shock.

"Fucking hell Princess." He coughs and gasps for air, his laughter finally stopping as he tightens his arms and starts moving us slowly to the music again. "Happiness and orgasms?"

"It's the two most important things in life! Wait, shit, no, I take that back. Coffee, coffee and orgasms are. Damn, I would kill someone for some coffee right now," I grumble. I asked Trev yesterday, but he informed me they can't grow it and you can't find it anymore. I am not too woman to admit that I teared up about that. Life on the run I can live with, but no coffee? It's a hard decision.

He rolls his eyes, but is still grinning. Not smirking or being a cocky crazy bastard, just grinning at me with happiness swirling in those ocean eyes. "What game did you want to play?" he asks, shaking his head like he forgot what we were talking about.

"Ohh yeah, you pick!" I say, moving with him as the music slows down on another song. He rolls his eyes to the ceiling, seeming to think. "Without using weapons, killing someone, torturing, or fire," I specify and he groans.

"That takes all the fun stuff away." He sighs and looks back at me. "Fine, what about Fuck, Kill, Eat?"

I blink at him, not sure what to say. "What is that?" I inquire. "So, we pick three people for each other and you pick the order

of what you would do to each of them." He smiles at me. "Here, I'll show you. Pick three people."

"I think I preferred I Spy," I mumble, but I turn my head and eye the crowd. "Okay, those three." I point out the chunky short man, a old grey haired woman, and a blonde middle-aged woman.

"Easy. Eat the fatty, more meat. Kill the oldie, cause she gonna die anyway, and fuck the blonde," he replies.

I grin up at him. "Your turn," I tell him, actually enjoying this game.

"Hmm, okay. Geeky dude, redhead, and oldie." He points them out and I giggle as I eye them.

"Fuck the redheaded woman, she has good tits. Kill the geek. Eat the oldie, it's like aged meat, right?" I look back to see him grinning at me, those dimples out again.

"Your crazy matches mine, you know that right?" he asks suddenly.

"Nuh-uh buddy, your crazy way outranks mine," I defend.

"Are we really going to argue about who is more crazy?" he counters, lowering his head so we are closer.

"You so are." I stick my tongue out at him.

"I'm not the one who pulled a fucking rock out of my own leg and killed a feral with it," he points out.

"Least I don't stalk people," I offer.

"I prefer to call it protective watching," he defends, making me laugh again. "You are beautiful," he says, before his eyes fly wide and his lips clamp shut like he didn't mean to tell me that.

Biting my lower lip, I try not to tease him...too much. "Is that right?" I smirk.

He rolls his eyes, but I watch as a cute blush flushes across his cheeks. "This is where you say, I'm pretty too," he jokes.

Tapping my chin, I step back and pretend to take him in from head to toe. "Well, I don't know—"

I laugh as he swoops in, picks me up, and swings me around. My hair flies out around my face and I can't stop laughing.

I guess there is beauty in the darkness, or to be more exact, beauty in the shadows.

Chapter 24
Meet The Tribe

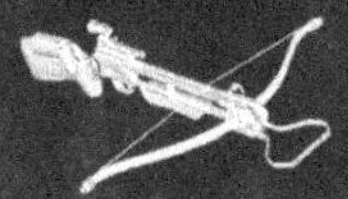

Thatnight, the moon and stars shine through the open window as I turn onto my back with a huff. I can't seem to sleep, everytime I close my eyes I fear what I will see. I'm irritating myself, which I don't like, I prefer to irritate other people.

Flopping to my side, I bury my hand under my pillow as I curl up tighter under the quilt. My eyes immediately seek out the area where I know Archel is, perched in his ever-present stalker chair. I can't hear him, or see him, but I know he is there. All it would take is for me to call out for him, and he would be at my side in an instant, but is that crossing a line with us? They are blurring and I don't know what we are to each other, but right now I need to be held and I promised myself I would live in the moment.

"Stalker?" I ask quietly, in case he is asleep. I know he needs his rest, he told me he is setting out at first light to make it across the Wastes in time.

He leans forward into the moon's rays so quickly that I jump a little. "What's wrong, Princess?" he growls, and when I look down I see his knives flash in the light.

"Sorry, I can't sleep," I finish lamely.

He snorts and puts away his weapons before getting to his feet.

He stops at the side of the bed and watches me.

"Will you stay with me?" I request and scoot backwards.

He looks from me to the bed before kicking off his boots and climbing on over the covers. I roll my eyes. "Dude, get the fuck under. I know you aren't going to feel me up."

He smiles but scoots under. "I was more worried about you feeling me up, I have to protect my virtue, you know," he mocks, making me grin.

He rolls to his side, until we are inches apart, his face turning serious. "Need me to fight your demons?" he murmurs softly.

Searching his eyes for the truth, I let my question flow out. "Would you?"

"I would fight Lucifer himself for you, I would follow you into your dreams and keep watch if I could. The best I can do is lie here, and ensure that you know that no one will ever touch you again. Not while I live," he vows.

"Why?" I ask, truly curious.

"I told you, you owe me," he mumbles, closing his eyes.

"Liar," I whisper and his lips twitch. He reaches out without looking and pulls me into his chest, tucking me close with his chin on my head.

"Sleep, Princess. I won't let the bad dreams get you, don't you know the shadows hide all? They can't touch you."

Closing my eyes, I bury my face in his chest and let him hold me for the night, fighting away those demons reaching for me so I can sleep, and I do. The whole night.

My eyes shoot open when something moves against me, my heart hammering and my palms turning sweaty as fear rushes through me. Unfocused, I blink, almost hyperventilating before a familiar, soothing voice reaches me.

"Shh, Princess. It's me."

Sucking in deep breaths, I slow down my heart and blink to clear my vision, finding Archel frozen with his arm half out from under me, where he must have been trying to sneak away without waking me. Relaxing, I close my eyes for a moment before opening them again.

"Sorry," I mutter and he shakes his head, cupping my cheek. "Never say sorry to me, I mean it. But I do have to go, if I don't go now I won't ever leave." He lays a gentle kiss on my forehead. "Stay out of trouble, Princess." He slides the rest of the way out and starts dressing as I watch sadly from the bed.

Finished dressing he walks away, stopping at the door. "Don't forget to practice, and if you can't sleep..." He shifts, rubbing the back of his head without looking at me. "I left you one of my shirts, I dunno, I thought it might help," he mumbles, and before I can open my mouth, he is gone and I'm alone again.

Shuffling, I bury myself in the warm spot he left behind, inhaling his scent. I lay there for a while before deciding to get up. I get dressed, the hut quiet without Archel's usual prodding. On his chair against the wall is my bow and katana, and a black shirt. Grin- ning, I inhale it before lying it back down and grabbing my weapons. I need to make my movements fluid and quick. A little part of me wants to impress him when he gets back, the other part of me just wants to shoot shit.

So I drag my ass to our clearing and set up. I spend hours just shooting bolts, trying new angles, reloading faster and pushing myself until I can reload in under five seconds and aim in less.

Once I am happyish, I move on to the katana, working through the moves he taught me and just feeling out the balance and move- ments. Archel told me once he got back we were going to sword fight, so I need to know how to move my feet in time with my slices.

The next time I take a break, the sun is high in the sky and sweat is pouring over me. It's probably about time for me to go meet Trev, so taking the katana as protection I quickly wash off in the stream and get dressed in fresh clothes. I drop the bow off at my hut but keep the katana on me, it makes me feel better.

Trev isn't at the clearing, so I look around, biting my lip before deciding to wander up the road to check the Hall. A couple are just leaving one of the houses as I walk past and they wave.

"Good morning!" they call and I smile at the friendly greeting. "Mornin, have you seen Trev at all?" I ask kindly.

"Sure thing sweetie, he's up at the tent dealing with any issues."

I nod and go to turn away when the woman calls again. "Have you had breakfast, Piper?"

"Erm, no?" I respond, unsure how she knows my name.

The man laughs and nudges her. "Sorry, everyone knows everyone here. You better get used to it, and just do what Martha here says, it's easier." He kisses her cheek and she pretends to smack him. He smiles at me before leaving and heading to the Hall.

"Come on, let's get some breakfast. He won't be free for a while." She grins.

Before I can object, she grabs my arm and starts wandering in the direction of the cooking area. Shrugging, I let her guide me. When we get there I see one of the tables has been turned into a breakfast area. She leads me to another close by and pushes me down before hurrying over to the other and grabbing two plates. I watch her in amusement as she starts filling them, smiling and talking to everyone on her way.

She hustles back over, dropping the plate in front of me as she sits opposite me.

"Thank you," I say, gratitude clear in my voice and she grins, her blue eyes lighting up with her smile. She's older than me, probably late fifties. Her blonde hair is brushed and straight, hanging over her rounded shoulders. She's not chubby, but curvy and I am already jealous of the dips her body has. The lines at her eyes and mouth tell me she smiles and laughs a lot.

"No problem, Piper. I know what it's like to be new, but everyone is nice around here and they will probably approach you now that your shadow has disappeared." She digs into her food and I do the same, chewing before I reply.

"What do you mean?" I ask, covering my mouth just incase. "Oh honey, don't get me wrong. He's fine as hell, but he is scary.

A lot of people give him a wide berth, and when he threatened to hang them by their entrails if they came near you or touch you— well, people listened."

I choke on my food and she leans over and pats my back. "He- he said that?" I cough, reaching for a drink and taking a sip.

"Yup, first night you came. We understood of course, the state you were in. It's obvious he was protecting you, so we let it be. But I would hope you would like to meet everyone?" she inquires, suddenly looking self-conscious.

Swallowing because that's the last fucking thing I want to do, I paste on a smile. "Of course, I just needed some time..."

She reaches over but stops before touching me. "We understand Piper. You do not need to explain," she finishes softly, a sad understanding in her eyes and that's when it hits me. They are all so happy because they have felt pain, Trev tried to explain but I didn't understand until now. She does understand, they all do because in some way or form this world has hurt them all.

More people flock over to our table as I mull over my new revelation. She introduces me to everyone, but names start to blur even as I smile and talk to them. When I've finished eating, I find myself relaxing in their midst as Martha tells a story to a young boy who is laughing along.

I eventually say goodbye and head back to the Hall. When I get there, I spot Trev talking to a bunch of people so I sidle up close and take a seat, happy to watch him work. If I am to help him, I need to know how this runs.

When he's finished talking, they leave happy and he makes his way over to me, a welcoming smile on his face. "I heard you were corralled into breakfast."

I grin, leaning back in the chair. "I had no choice, Martha was involved." He nods as he sits down, a sigh escaping him.

"Everyday, morning to noon, I am here for any concerns, complaints, and patrol meetings. If you choose to help me, I would love to have you here with me. In the afternoon, I either patrol or go on the hunts. Every member of our tribe works in some capacity."

I nod, taking it all in. "It would be patrol for me," I answer automatically, surprising myself. It seems *they* couldn't ruin my love and eagerness to be out there, helping, protecting.

"Okay, so let's go through some current issues." He turns to me and I listen intently as he outlines issues the tribe presently faces, while explaining some rules and how the hierarchy is set out.

I am entranced and hours later, I am still talking with the tribe leader, learning from him.

Chapter 25
Returning Angel

I spend my days with Trev and my afternoons on patrol. I don't go far at first, Simon and I stay closer to the camp until I am comfortable with the terrain, and then we venture farther.

He shows me where they collect water, and the location of the hunting fields. He also shows me the escape routes in and out. They even have some through the mountain, I peered into the dark hole but it gave me the shivers so I moved on fast. When I asked if anyone could get through, he told me nothing exists on the other side... just barren.

I soak up all the knowledge like a sponge, I even watch the way he walks because for such a big man he sure is silent. I try copying him and once he catches me he shows me how to move in near silence.

My days are so busy that at night I sleep like the dead, curled up in Archel's shirt. The smell of it helps settle me, and even once when I woke up in a cold sweat, I felt like he was here with his scent lingering on me and the sheets. I have also started getting up early and running again, before training with my bow and katana. My body is almost fully recovered now. I don't get tired halfway through the day and besides the random twinge of my leg every now and again, I can start to build my strength and stamina back up.

Before I know it, the five days are up.

I am just walking through a section of the trees, checking the snares and traps when I hear a familiar sounding motorcycle roaring towards us. I grin over at Simon and he jerks his head towards the road that Archel will be coming in from. My smile only grows, and I salute at him before I take off in the direction of the road, moving through the trees and traps with ease, and step out of the tree line as my shadow rounds the corner like some kind of angel, the sun haloed behind him.

He roars to a stop, kicking out the stand as he sits on the idle bike. He grins over at me and I beam back. Stepping closer I hesi- tate at his side.

"What, too good for a fucking hug, Princess?" he mocks.

Sticking my tongue out at him I move into his open arms and he wraps them around me, pulling me close. I hear him sigh and I feel the same way, I guess as much as I didn't want to admit it, I was terri- fied he wouldn't come back. I can thank my parents for abandonment issues. I breathe in his scent, content to be in his arms. He feels like home and safety and maybe even a little happiness.

"Did you bring me a present?" I ask, my voice muffled by his chest, but I feel it when he laughs, shaking against me.

"Hop on, Princess." Pulling back from his chest I roll my eyes at him, but I swing my leg over the seat behind him and hold on to his waist as he kicks off and roars into the camp. He goes straight to our hut before stopping again. I get off and he grabs his bag from the back of the bike.

I follow him inside, almost bouncing on my toes.

"Never thought I would say I missed this fucking room," he grumbles, and flops back on the bed, the bag on the floor by his feet. Frowning, I take him in. He's covered in sand and blood and looks exhausted. His eyes are shadowed, his face pale. "What happened?" I demand, stepping between his parted thighs.

He opens his eyes, wearily looking at me. "Same shit, different day."

"Archel," I warn and he grins at me, those fucking dimples of his peeking out.

"I love the way you say my name, like you don't know whether to kiss me or kick me." He laughs and my mouth drops open as I sputter. "Relax, Princess. I'm fine. Was just a hard ride, we are on the opposite side on the Wastes and I encountered a few Berserkers that I had to deal with." He closes his eyes and I narrow mine. "Come here," he mutters without even looking at me.

Crossing my arms, I glare at him. He peeps one eye open and smirks when he sees me. Lightning fast, he darts up and grabs me, sending me tumbling onto his chest. Humming, he wraps his arms around me as he sighs.

Eventually, I relax. "Are you okay?" I ask, concerned.

"Nothing I couldn't handle, but Princess? I need to leave again in three days. Shit is going down. I can feel it in the wind." He sounds so concerned that I can't be mad.

Pushing up, I look down at him as he tangles our legs. "Then I come with you."

He shakes his head sadly, and cups my cheek. "No, you are needed here and I wouldn't be able to concentrate with you there. I will be back, I just need to find out some information."

"Promise?" I whisper, not liking it but knowing he is right, I would only hinder him.

"Always, I will always come back to you Piper." We share a soft caring look. "Besides, who is going to play Fuck, Kill, Eat with you?"

I laugh and he leans up, and I freeze when he drops a soft kiss on my lips. Not pushing, just gentle. "Couldn't resist," he murmurs against my lips and pulls back, searching my face. "I have wanted to do that since the first time I saw you."

"When I was holding a gun to you?" I joke and he laughs. "Yes," he confirms.

Dropping my head to his chest, I lie there in his arms. "Crazy bastard," I mutter and he grins, sweeping his lips over my forehead.

"What did I miss, tell me everything," he insists, and I thought I missed this jerk...okay I did...like a tiny bit. Teeny tiny. But I tell him everything, he would only go and beat it out of someone else if I didn't.

We spend the rest of the afternoon just relaxing and catching up and before I know it, it's time for the evening meal. I grab his hand and drag him with me, vowing to let him have an early night, but I know I need to go or Martha or Simon will come looking for me. They don't let me wallow or hide.

We find our normal spots on the ground to eat quietly as I watch people. Simon drops a drink nearby for me and Martha toddles over and makes sure I have enough to eat.

"Seems like you have made some friends," he comments, leaning back on his arms. Dropping my now empty plate I lean back on his arm and watch the fire dance.

"You told me not to get into trouble," I point out and he snorts.

He goes quiet after that, and I leave him to his thoughts knowing how tired he is. Instead, we continue to watch everyone. Trev wanders over at some point and welcomes him back, but he is the only one who does.

"Come on, you need to wash and get some sleep," I order, getting to my feet and looking down at him.

He grins up at me as he stretches out, his muscles straining against his shirt. "So bossy, Princess. Are you going to wash my back?"

Ignoring him, I turn and I hear him get up and follow. I go to head back to the hut but he grabs my hand and tugs me after him, through the trees and to the pond.

"Can't let you wander alone, you attract trouble," he teases before pushing me down on the water's edge. I sit cross-legged as he starts to strip. Last week I would have averted my gaze, last month I would have made a rude joke. This time? I take in my fill.

I drink in every tight muscle, each a hard line. He's like a machine, all perfect edges, not an inch of fat. He's not as big as Jago but he sure as fuck looks just as perfect.

He lets me look before he turns and wades into the water, luckily still in his boxers. He ducks under, slicking back his hair as he scrubs the dirt and blood from his body. I find myself gawking, watching him, and as my pussy starts to pulse I nearly fall into the water in shock. Fucking hell, I thought that bitch was dead for good, but nope, here she is getting all hot and bothered over the wet assassin.

Most people wouldn't be thinking about sex again, but we have already established I am crazy and that everyone heals at different rates. It doesn't mean I'm ready to jump him, but it's a step in the right direction. Everybody aboard the sex train, choo choo.

Oblivious to my dirty thoughts, Archel gets out and dries off, washing his clothes and draping them over his arm. "Come on, let's head back."

I nod, trying and failing not to stare at his semi hard cock through the wet fabric of his boxers, which are clinging to it nicely. "Have you named your cock?" I ask, genuinely curious and he mutters something before letting out a pained noise.

"Please stop saying cock and staring at mine, we both know you aren't ready for that, and if you keep looking at me this way I am going to have to kill myself for touching you," he grits out.

Pulling my eyes up his washboard abs, I catch the pained grimace on his face and decide to take it easy on him. "Come on, stalker, I'm tired."

He follows me back to the hut, which is a good idea or I would just be eyeing up his arse. I strip off my jeans and boots, leaving on my shirt as I crawl into bed without looking at him, wanting to give him some privacy and time for me to control my hormones.

Facing the wall, I feel the bed shift as he climbs in and pulls me to him, his skin cold but now dry. "Goodnight, Princess."

"Night," I whisper back.

"Don't forget, training bright and early. Let me see what you learned," he jibes.

Groaning, I bury my head into my pillow to hide my smile that quirks up my lips anyway.

Chapter 26
Presents

Archel woke me up crazy early and dragged me to our usual training ground. When he saw that I had actually been practising and he witnessed my new skills with the bow, he was impressed. We then practiced with the katana, he even grabbed one and started parrying with me before he taught me how to attack with it, and where to cut to disable my enemy the fastest.

Panting, I drop the katana as he steps back, looking me over. "Colour me impressed, Princess. Guess I better give you your presents."

"Presents?" I clap, dropping the sword and launching myself at him.

He catches me mid-air, laughing before he drops a kiss on my lips. We both freeze, me dangling in his arms with our lips connected.

He pulls back, his eyes cast down. "Sorry Piper, I didn't mean to catch you off guard like that, I—"

I shut him up by kissing him. He groans, the sound reverberating through me and I pull back, my breath hitching as I hook my legs around his waist.

"Piper," he pants, watching me with concerned eyes, but I don't want his concern.

Leaning forward, I peck his lips. He is as still as a statue while I kiss his cheek and his nose, then back to his lips. When he doesn't kiss me back, I bite his lower lip and he bursts to life. Gripping the back of my head, he wraps my hair around his fist and tugs my head back until it strains my neck. Covering my lips, he bites and licks until I open, and he sweeps his tongue in. Groaning into his mouth, I give as good as I get, tasting him.

Pulling back, we both stare at each other as we breathe heavily. Swallowing, I kiss him once more before dropping my legs from his waist. He lets me go, unwinding my hair from his fist.

"Let me get your presents," he mutters, wincing as he reaches down and rearranges his cock which is pressing against the front of his jeans.

Turning, he grabs his bag and starts rooting around before he pulls out a crossbow. He passes it to me with a grunt and I stare at it in awe. Painted red with flames on the side, it has a bolt holder underneath with a fancy new black sheen.

"Oh my God, I love it!" I gush and he grins before digging back in his bag.

He pulls out an old silver container and I frown, eyeing him.

"I found some guy who swears he blends coffee. Now, I don't know what it's going to be like, but I figured it was worth a shot." He thrusts it at me.

"You... bought... me... coffee?" I drawl slowly.

He nods, looking everywhere but at me. Squealing I drop everything to the ground and fly at him again. Peppering kisses over his face I whisper my thanks.

"Alright, don't get all mushy on me Princess," he mutters, even as he grins at me, those ocean eyes sparkling.

We have dinner with Trev who goes over any issues in the tribe I missed this morning while I was training. We agree on solutions and then I head out for patrol with my new crossbow strapped to my back, my sword at my hip, and Archel by my side. I walk the same route Simon showed me, going the long way around to prolong my time with him.

We check all the traps, like Simon taught me, and I grab a rabbit from one. Archel slings it over his shoulder as we scout in silence. Only once we are back to the camp do we talk.

I drop the rabbit with the people who have already starting cooking and head back to the hut to get dressed for the meal. Archel and I work seamlessly side by side, not needing words.

It isn't until we sit down to eat that night when I realise we both haven't spoken in hours. Even then though, I don't feel the need to break the silence. It's comfortable, but I do anyway because I need some questions answered.

"So when do you leave?" I ask sadly.

"Tomorrow morning, I don't know how long I will be gone for," he warns, wrapping an arm around my shoulders and dragging me to his side.

"But you will be back," I conclude and he kisses my shoulder. "Look, you are learning, Princess," he taunts.

"Cockwanker," I reply and he laughs.

"I'm going to miss you, Princess," he whispers, and I barely hear him over the laughter and talking of the rest of the tribe.

Looking over my shoulder I meet his serious eyes. "I'm going to miss you too," I admit.

We stare at each other, both lost in each other's eyes until Martha hustles over and breaks it up.

The rest of the night is a blur, I never want it to end but people start drifting off to bed, so reluctantly I do too. When we get to our hut I strip and get under the covers, Archel following after. Turning over, our noses nearly touching, I watch him as he watches me.

"Look after yourself Princess," he demands. "Shut up," I fire back.

"Trust Trev, don't venture too far out—"

"Shut up," I repeat loudly, covering his mouth with my finger. "This sounds far too much like goodbye and I have had enough of those to last me a lifetime. So no matter what you find out there, you fight through it all. You fight and you come back to me," I order.

"Yes, Princess. As you command." He grins and I nod, wishing I could ask him to stay, wishing he would.

Chapter 27
Light Of Day

The morning comes too soon, and for once I want to fight the rays lighting up the sky and guiding us home. I awoke early, when it was still dark, and I just watched him. He looks so peaceful in his sleep, long black lashes fanned against his cheeks, stubble covering his chin from not shaving, hair in disarray. I wanted to reach out and touch him, but I knew if I did he would wake up and then he would leave. When he does wake, his smile is sleepy. He kisses me good morning, but I refuse to let him move. Just holding on for two more minutes before he sighs and gets up.

Archel kisses me goodbye, softly like he is savouring it, before swinging onto his bike and roaring away without another look back. Straightening my shoulders I march straight to the Hall, ready to start the day. The busier I am, the less I will worry.

That day I lose myself in tasks. I help cook the food and I am really bad at it. I help mend houses, clothes, and fences. I go on patrol and I practice my crossbow, but when it gets dark and I am in bed all alone, my mind turns to the three men who I miss.

Who knew someone was capable of caring for three men at once? I guess it is only like a mother loving all her children though. Closing my eyes, I bring the images of Jago, Evan, and Archel to mind, imagining them here as I fall asleep.

I miss you.

The days go by in a blur, with each passing one I get stronger, faster, and more capable. I learn more of the tribe's history and the people who call this home. I spend my days with Trev and eat my meals with the whole tribe. They accept me with open arms and begin coming to me with problems. Whenever I point that out, Trev only smiles and nods knowingly.

I worked myself hard today, training for hours followed by scouting and patrol for another six or seven hours, but when I get to bed that night, nothing I do will make me sleep. I knew it was going to be a bad day when I woke up, I could just feel it. Doesn't help that Archel has been gone for two weeks, two weeks with no word or sign of the assassin. I even see Trev start to worry. Thoughts swirling and heart squeezing tight, I get dressed in the dark, strapping on my katana and crossbow like I do every morning and head outside.

Walking the perimeter, I ensure all the torches lighting camp are still burning, and then I circle back to my training area. Once there, I start shooting at the already set up target, losing myself in the rhythmic pull and release of the bow, the bolts whizzing through the air and embedding in the target.

Sighing, I walk forward and pluck them from the bullseye, ready to go again when I hear a strange sound. Frowning, I tilt my head and listen harder. It comes again, it sounds like...running feet.

Backing away from the trees, I almost scream when the moonlight catches the whites of the creature's eyes lurking at the tree line where I just was. I watch in dawning horror as its mouth opens wide, showing its pointed teeth and it lets out a spine shivering growl. More creatures echo the growl from inside the dense dark- ness, making me tremble.

Panic builds in me, but I push it down. I know I need to warn the others, and try and get everyone to safety, there is no time for fear and panic now. Losing one bolt directly at its face, I turn and sprint back to camp. I hear it yowl before the sound of growls and screams meets me, running footsteps sounding on the ground as they nip at my heels.

Reaching the torches lighting the way, I cup my hand over my mouth.

"EATERS!" I scream at the top of my lungs. There is a commotion as the patrols and scouts hear my yells. "EATERS!" I scream again to be sure, and it ends on a shout as I tumble to the ground, something on top of me, its clawed hand gripping my leg where it yanked me down.

Flipping over, I kick at its ugly, mottled face. Grabbing my crossbow I shoot at the others trying to sneak past me, trying to buy the tribe time. The one at my ankle bites into my leg, making me scream in agony.

It shakes it like a dog on a bone before letting go. Its mouth drips with my blood as it grins at me.

"You ugly motherfucker, don't you know you have to ask if people like bite play?" I yell before shooting it right in the fucking eye.

The bolt sticks from its eye as its head jerks back from the impact. Its hand loosens on my ankle as it tumbles to the side. Reaching down I pluck out the bolt, ignoring the horrible sound it makes as I pull it free. Pushing to my feet, I wince as I hop, trying to ignore the pain ripping through my leg. Two more circle me as another jumps on it's fallen comrade and starts ripping through its flesh.

Grimacing, I drag my eyes back to the other two as they dart in and try to bite me.

"What the hell is it with all the biting, anyone would think you are zombies!" I yell, exasperated as I reload my crossbow. When they move closer I sling it over my shoulder and grab my katana, thanking myself for strapping up before I went for a walk.

The one to my left leaps at me, I spin like Archel taught me, slashing out with my sword across its stomach. I gag when I cut through its flesh, its intestines falling out as it lands on its side, whimpering. Alternating between whining and growling, it climbs to its feet, wobbling as things that shouldn't be outside of its stomach, are.

"That's fucking nasty," I comment. I yelp and raise the katana as the other leaps at me. I fall back to the ground, the blade caught in its teeth as it tries to rip my face off.

"Hey bitch, that's the fucking money maker!" I yell before raising my uninjured leg and kicking him off.

He flies backwards and I jump to my feet, almost collapsing from the pain in my leg. My head spins and I bite my lip to hold in the scream wanting to erupt from my throat. Grunting, I push forward and before it can get to its feet again, I grab the straggly locks of hair remaining on its head, pull back, and slit its throat.

Letting go, it tumbles to the floor and I turn to the other one, which is now trying to drag its way to me.

"Really man? I gotta give you points for determination." Rolling my shoulders, I limp over and raise my sword.

"I feel like I should say something really cool or dramatic right now, but you caught me off guard so...rest in peace, bitch," I say before hacking at its neck.

Sure they are dead, I limp back towards the camp. I see the fires going and people milling about. Guards and patrols are brandishing weapons and firing into the night at the eaters attacking. The unarmed and untrained civilians are running down main street, heading for the tent where Trev stands guard, an assault rifle in his hand as he fires into the darkness, a fierce look on his face.

Gritting my teeth, I ignore the fire burning my leg and the blood drenching my ripped pants and boot, and head his way intent on helping. I cry out when an eater flies from behind a hut and grabs a woman, throwing her into the trees before being hit with an array of bullets from guards.

I hear the gurgled scream of the woman as the eaters waiting there rip into her. Fucking hell. Picking up the pace I meet the first guard who is slowly walking backwards, keeping watch as they retreat.

I grab his arm, stilling his movement. His frantic eyes lock on mine, his face is pale and sweating, and I can almost smell the fear wafting from him. "We need to push them back, let the others get to the tent. Come on, if we don't kill them they will only keep coming!" I yell over the sounds of gunfire and he nods reluctantly.

Waving my hand over my head I catch Trev's attention. Cupping my mouth, I shout as loud as I can to be heard. "We will push them back, get everyone inside!"

He nods, stepping forward as he shouts for people to get in. I grab some more guards and patrols, getting them to pass the message down the line about pushing back. We form a line in front of the tent, side by side as the last civilians get inside. It goes quiet, deadly quiet, until the growling starts up again.

"Shoot low, hit fast, and move on. Don't let them get too close. Whatever you do, don't break the line!" I warn and I hear a chorus of agreements.

They scurry out from the trees, obviously realising we are too far away. There are too many to count, over thirty at least. I hear the men's breathing, feel their fear as we stand together, facing down death. Yet I've never felt more alive, even as fear races through me, but maybe that fear is good, it might keep me from dying.

They all launch at once, flying through the air, teeth snapping, saliva dripping, and we yell back. Shots are fired, striking them mid-air, many fall but some keep coming. I take aim, shooting bolt after bolt, killing at least five before I have to sling it over my shoulder and wait with my sword. They leap from the ground on all fours, like lions running as they near us.

Steadying my breathing, I push off and slide beneath the one coming straight at me. I slip under it, cutting as I go and turn to another, cutting across its neck as I turn back to the first and impale it on my sword.

I have to duck as gunfire sounds and I turn to find a man screaming, going down with one of them ripping at his throat. Blood squirts everywhere as he carries on shooting. Moving as fast as I can, I scream as I fling my body at the eater on top of him. We fall to the ground, the wind knocked out of me, and it's on me quicker than I can move. Grunting, I batter its head with the pummel until he growls and backs away. Sliding backwards, I search the slick ground until I meet warm, wet sticky skin, ignoring that, I grab the gun and take aim.

Firing, I watch its body twitch as the bullets rip holes through it.

Satisfied it is dead, I push to my feet and look around. Only a few more remain, some slink away into the night, and others are being taken care of. Leaning heavily on the gun, I check over everyone. Two men lie on the ground.

"Simon!" I yell and he runs from the tent, covered in blood. "Sorry! Was trying to save—" He shakes his head and makes his way to the men. I watch his back, making sure nothing else sneaks out.

"Get them inside," I order and two men help him get the deathly still men inside.

"Okay, we keep watch. I don't know if they will be back, but better safe than sorry. We don't leave until the sun rises!" I yell. They agree as we reform our line, ready to face down anything that emerges from the light, the last line of defense.

I stand there for hours, not moving. My eyes twitching as I concentrate on the tree line. The people inside are vulnerable, I have to protect them, so that's what I do. When the first rays of sun start to ripple through the sky I sigh in relief. We made it through the night, but what horror awaits us in the light of day?

Chapter 28
Goodbye

Groaning, I lean back on the bed, raising my foot like Simon ordered. I had been limping around camp, helping move bodies and bury the dead. I left Trev to reassure people, that wasn't my forte, but when Simon had found me, he grabbed me and carried me back to my hut. He placed me on the bed and treated my wounds, he started to fuss and I demanded he go and see to everyone else—I know I am not the only injured one. He left reluctantly, placing my weapons near me just in case.

I almost laugh when I hear the motorbike roaring towards me. I hear it skid to a stop outside before Archel is filling the doorway. A sword held in both hands as his desperate eyes seek me out. When he does, his shoulders drop and he sheathes the sword.

Striding towards me, he doesn't stop until he is sitting next to me. "What happened?"

"Just some eaters," I mutter, leaning back with a wince. He takes me in, twisting my arms and raising my top until he gets to my bandaged leg.

"Princess. I saw the fucking bodies, that wasn't some," he countered.

211

"Nothing to worry about," I reply tiredly, my eyes almost sliding shut, he must notice because he sighs.

"Sleep, I will keep watch and we can talk about it when you wake up."

I try to nod but I am already sliding into oblivion.

"Why do you always get hurt when I'm not here?" He sighs, rewrapping my leg for me. It feels worse than it looks, and luckily Simon had some drugs to prevent infection on hand. He said the next twenty-four hours are critical, if infection sets in there isn't much they can do. He offered to cut off my leg, I told him to go fuck himself.

"I guess you'll just have to stick with me all the time," I quip back.

"Your shadow," he mocks and we both laugh.

"Princess—" He starts, before looking away, and something in his voice has me sitting up straighter.

"What is it? Are you okay? Did something happen?" I ask rapid-fire.

"No, well yes, something happened," he stutters, twining his hand with mine.

I take in his dejected and tired expression and slump. "You are leaving again?" I conclude.

He looks up, nodding. "Not forever, I swear. I will tell you everything, but it's better that Trev hears all of it too. I came back to bring you with me, but..."

We both look at my leg, there is no way I am riding, never mind leaving camp.

"I understand," I say softly and he grips my hand tighter. "Princess."

"Really, Archel. It's fine. I've managed without you for this long, I can for a bit longer."

He looks away and I squeeze his hand before letting go. "We

better go and tell Trev then, whatever it is sounds important. Plus, I need to check on everyone."

He stands mutely and scoops me up into his arms, holding me there as we leave the hut and head to the tent. I take in the devastation and bloodshed left behind from the attack. All of the tables and chairs lay on their side, splattered with blood and other stains. The logs remain forgotten as well, and the fire is nothing but smoldering ashes. Eater bodies are piled near the exit to camp, they are throwing them there before they take them off to burn so they don't rot and stink up everything. Four new graves sit under a particularly large tree, each a reminder of what we lost last night.

When we reach the tent I see a haggard looking Trev. Simon has set up a triage to one side and the amount of wounded astounds me. Archel heads straight to Trev. One look at our faces and he excuses himself from the conversation he was in, and we head to one corner.

"Good to see you back, but I take it that it is not good news?" he inquires, getting straight to the point.

"I'm afraid not. The Berserker clan has started a war, a Summit is being called. Dray has asked me to collect an important person and be at his back for it. After it is done I will be back. I don't know what this means for you old friend, but I do know that hiding and hoping for the best won't work anymore. I wish I could stay and help you, but I need you to protect Piper."

I go to protest but he ignores me. "I know she can protect herself, but I swear to you old man. If anything happens to her, I will kill you all myself," he states casually, but from the look on Trev's face, he knows he isn't kidding.

"I will help you sort this mess out, then I must leave. I have brought more weapons and some food for you to store," he adds, seeming to deflate now that he has got it all out.

"What's going on?" I ask, not understanding most of the conversation.

"War, Piper. The Wastes are going to war," Trev says sadly.

Sucking in a breath, I blow it out slowly. "Okay, we are hidden here but that doesn't mean much. We need to step up patrols and extend the border. We need to train everyone to be able to protect themselves and set more traps. We need back up plans and more escape routes. I suggest through the mountain, the fighters will be coming the other way...." I trail off at both of their incredulous expressions. "What?"

"Nothing, Princess. I just forget sometimes how smart you are."

Glaring at him I turn to Trev. "We can do it, but I will need your help. My leg will hinder me for a while, except we can't wait."

He nods and smiles at me, a sad one with a shared understanding. We both came here for a fresh start and it seems they are threatening our dream now. I guess that means we fight.

The sun is high in the sky as the smoke from the eater bonfire finally floats away. We have a small goodbye ceremony for the dead, and I lean against Archel determined to stand. As the ceremony concludes, everyone slowly breaks away, mourning. I remain behind with Archel.

"You have to leave now, don't you?" I ask sadly, staring at the graves. I have a feeling before this war is out there will be a lot more than just these four.

"Yes," he answers softly, dropping his chin onto my shoulder as he holds me.

"You should go, it's important, Archel. I will be here when you get back."

"What if you aren't?" he growls, tightening his arms around me. "I will, if I'm not here we will meet in the mountains. You can find me anywhere, right stalker?" I tease, turning in his arms to look up at him.

"I don't want to leave, Princess. I want to stay, with you. I've never felt like that. I've always done my duty, followed Dray's orders. He's my brother, my best friend, but right now I want to ignore all of that and stay. Tell me to and I will. Tell me to stay," he pleads, searching my face.

Looking down, I gather my thoughts before leaning into him harder. "I want to, I really do, but that would be selfish. He needs you, the Wastes need you. I won't ask you to stay, but I will order you to come back." My breath hitches as I try to hold everything back.

He cups my cheek and presses a gentle kiss on my lips. "Until next time, Princess. Try to stay out of trouble," he warns and we both laugh, the sound choked and filled with emotions.

Dropping his hand from my cheek he spins and heads back to his bike. "Archel!" I shout and he turns.

I limp over to him and he meets me halfway, his hands going to my hips as our lips come together in a desperate kiss.

A goodbye.

"Give them hell," I whisper against his mouth.

He nods, kissing me again. I keep my eyes closed, not wanting to see him leave again, not when he wanted to stay. When I finally blink them open, all that is left is a sand cloud where he once was.

Goodbye, my shadow.

Chapter 29

A Beast And A Tribe

It's been two days since the attack, two days since I sent Archel back into a war zone. I spent the time sorting out the defenses, and Trev actually listens to me as we put new plans and curfews in place. No one goes out alone, everyone carries a weapon, and everyone must learn to protect themselves. We have planned a tribe meeting for later today to announce all of this. Simon and I also scouted farther out than any Forgotten tribe member ever has, and planned where we could lay new traps and trip wires. Things that will give us enough warning in case anything comes again. We can't face a night like the attack again, it crippled us and only made us more aware that these people came here for peace not war—but that doesn't seem to be an option for us anymore. If what Archel says is true, and my gut tells me to believe him, we might not have a choice any longer. Every night I stare at the stars and beg whoever is still out there to protect him, to make sure he finds this person fast and makes it back to whatever this

Summit is. All so he can come back here—come back to me.

Sighing, I shake my head free of my thoughts as I leave the Hall. I have a lot still left to do today and my leg is killing me. We don't have painkillers like in Paradise, and once we knew I was over the infection, all we could do is try and let it heal. I can bear weight now, but I think I will always have a wicked looking scar from it. Simon continues to tell me off when he sees me up and about, but I know we don't have time to spare.

So I slowly make my way back to my hut for a little bit of alone time, maybe to even rest my leg, before all hell breaks loose. I hear a noise from the road, and faster than I can blink, my katana is in my hand, ready for any attack. All my fatigue and plans are forgotten as adrenaline surges through my body.

When the attack I am expecting or shouts don't come, I look up and freeze, the weapon dropping to the ground from my shock. There, in the middle of the road, is Jago. My Beast, the man who showed me a life above ground, the man who has my heart even though he doesn't know it. The man I left behind. Here, in The Forgotten.

We are just staring at each other from meters away. His face is hard and covered in blood, probably not his own. He watches me like he's seeing a ghost and I do the same. He strides towards me where I stand frozen. My katana hangs at his side, the one he gave me, not the one from Archel, and I don't know what to say—so as usual my smart mouth opens.

"I spy something beginning with J," I gasp out, my voice shaking. I want to reach out and touch him and make sure he's real, that the pain isn't getting to me or that this isn't a dream. That my Beast is really here, that he really came for me.

"Shut up, Brawler," he orders, before dropping everything and striding towards me, closing that last bit of distance between us. He picks me up in one swoop and drags me to his chest as his lips cover mine. He shows me his desperation, his relief, and his love, and when I pull away to breathe I drop my forehead to his. His fire eyes are roaring and I can't look away, if I do he might disappear even as my lips tingle from his touch. I rove my eyes over his face, drinking him in. God, I missed him so much.

"I have been looking fucking everywhere for you," he growls.

"I thought we were playing a new game, hide and seek," I quip, making him grunt out a hysterical laugh.

"Fuck, I missed you so much Brawler. Even that smart fucking mouth of yours," he whispers, his eyes swimming with emotion, the same ones I am betting are reflected in mine. I never thought I would see him again. I hoped, but logically I knew it was unlikely. It seems this world still has some surprises left in store for me. You don't fuck with what a beast wants, because he will always push back.

"Only cause you missed it sucking your cock," I tease and he shakes his head, serious all of a sudden. Just then tribesmen step out from behind the trees, all weapons pointed at Jago. He growls and drops me to the ground and pulls me behind him.

"Wait!" I shout as I push away and step in front of him. "He's a friend. I swear! Lower your weapons," I order, and surprisingly they do. I turn back to Jago, seeing the confusion on his face.

"What happened to you?" I ask, taking him in from head to toe. Blood and bruises cover him and he looks like he hadn't showered or eaten for weeks.

"What's going on, Brawler?" he demands in that voice he used when he was training me. The one that commanded my attention and obedience, not that it worked. His eyes flicker to the tribesmen with guns, no doubt taking in their weakness and stance, and forming a plan of attack.

"Welcome to The Forgotten," I say dramatically, sweeping my hand out to encompass my new home.

Epilogue

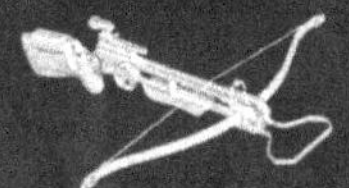

Jago follows me to my hut, glaring at anyone who comes close. Once inside, I finish getting ready for the meeting as I pepper him with questions, needing to understand how he is here right now even as my heart bursts from seeing him again.

"Did Evan come with you?" I ask with my back to him, so he can't see the hope and longing in my eyes.

He's quiet for a moment before his arms wrap around me from behind, and I melt into him. "No, he started going out on patrol to look for you. I went alone."

Spinning, I stare at him in shock. "Evan went on patrol?"

"Yep, guess he finally found his balls. I haven't been back in over a month though, so I'm not sure where he is now," Jago deadpans, has it really been that long? I guess I lost track of time, but who needs it out here? One day blends into the next. Our moment is broken when I hear raised voices from the community, making me swear.

The fucking meeting. As much as I want to melt into Jago's arms and forget everything and just let him hold me like old times, I have responsibilities now. I hope he understands.

"Brawler, what's going on?" he demands, proving he always sees too much.

"There's a meeting being held to discuss the attacks on the Waste and the Summit that's been called," I reply tiredly.

"What are you talking about?" he questions in frustration. "Archel, the guy who helped us at the house, is part of the Seekers and he left and came back with some information, information that means we need to be ready. The tribe is going to meet as we speak," I explain, unsure how to describe everything that has happened. It feels like a lifetime ago since I saw him and I have too much to cover and too little time.

"I think you better start from the top Brawler, and don't leave anything out," he orders.

Sighing, I eye the door but nod, he deserves this after carving a bloody path through the Wastes looking for me. I just hope he doesn't see me differently when he learns what happened. That would break my heart.

"They told me you were dead," he growls, but I see the pain in his eyes, blending with the anger in his voice.

"I was, I nearly was. Archel saved me," I reply softly.

He backs me into the bed, caging me there. "Who do I need to kill?" he grits out through clenched teeth.

"No one, I did it already. But I have a feeling there will be a lot more killing to come. If you stay..." I trail off, suddenly unsure.

"I go wherever you are Brawler, I thought that was obvious." He rolls his eyes at me.

I grin. "I knew you liked me, it was the boobs right?"

He groans but lowers his head to mine. "Shut up, Brawler." He drops a gentle kiss on my lips and lifts his head again.

"Now, what happened?"

So I open my mouth and everything spills out. I don't know what is going to happen, I don't know where the other part of my hearts are, and I tremble in fear knowing that both of them are out there. But one thing is for sure. With Jago by my side and Archel at my back, no one will hurt me ever again. I'll make sure of it. The Beast, the Shadow, the Doctor. It sounds like a weird start to a joke, not my love life, but I wouldn't have it any other way.

We had to hurry to the meeting, my rundown of everything taking so much time. I can see the fury in Jago and I feel it in his body as he touches me, never letting go. I skipped some of the gory details of what happened to me, I told him everything else. Every single detail because it's Jago and he wouldn't let me do otherwise, but I also never want to lie to him. Our time apart has only shown me how much I need him. How much I miss him. How much I care for him. I know he isn't the type to forget, but I have too much else to deal with right now so I keep some of the little things out, planning to tell him later on when we are alone.

The meeting goes as you could expect. People are angry, people want answers, they are confused and scared, and it's mine and Trev's job to calm and reassure them. We explain our plans and when we reach an agreement, I let my shoulders slump. Jago has been by side ever since, his hands on me like if he isn't touching me I will disappear.

I tell Trev to let everyone rest today, but tomorrow we start training. He nods and we dismiss the meeting. Getting up, I lean on Jago as we make our way from the tent.

"Thank you," says a smaller familiar man as he steps in my path. "You saved my life." I nod and smile, stepping around him.

People start to gather around us as we try to leave. "Thank you, Piper."

"She saved us."

I ignore it all, I'm grateful for their praise but it's not why I did it. They are my family now, family protects one another.

We leave the tent, slowly walking down the dirt road, when a commotion comes from the edge of the trees.

Groaning, I look up at the sky. "What now," I mumble.

A scout breaks the tree line, panting, and covered in blood. He bends over, dry heaving as more tribe members gather around.

"What is the meaning of this, are you okay?" Trev shouts, pushing through the crowd.

"An attack, sir. Attack." He coughs, gasping for breath and I stiffen.

"Attack? Attack where?" Trev asks as murmurs run through the crowd.

"Paradise, sir. Paradise has fallen."

Reader Advisory

As promised in my first note, here are the triggers featured in this book. If you feel I have missed any, please do not hesitate to reach out.

- Violence is prevalent throughout this book as is bloodshed.
- Rape, there is a scene where the main character is raped. It does fade to black but it does contain some graphic details.

Acknowledgments

I'll try to keep this short and sweet, like me...well the short part anyway! This book took on a life of its own and I am so thankful to all the wonderful people standing behind me urging me on.

To Meg, thank you for reading the hard bits and reassuring me people won't hate me...to much. To MalMal, you are a star and I don't know how you manage to keep me organised. To Jess and Kaila, you took my ramblings and made them flow. To my betas, Jess F, Jess M, Harley, Andrea, Sam, Kristen, April, Kala, who took this crazy journey with me, I love you.

Lastly, my readers. Your support and love keeps me writing and I wouldn't be here without you.

Thank you for following me down the forgotten, if you enjoyed this book, please leave a review. It would really help!

Katie

About K.A. Knight

K.A. Knight is an USA Today bestselling indie author trying to get all of the stories and characters out of her head, writing the monsters that you love to hate. She loves reading and devours every book she can get her hands on, and she also has a worrying caffeine addiction.

She leads her double life in a sleepy English town, where she spends her days writing like a crazy person.

Read more at K.A. Knight's website or join her Facebook Reader Group.
Sign up for exclusive content and my newsletter here
http://eepurl.com/drLLoj

Also by K.A. Knight

THEIR CHAMPION SERIES *Dystopian RH*

The Wasteland

The Summit

The Cities

The Nations

Their Champion Coloring Book

Their Champion - the omnibus

The Forgotten

The Lost

The Damned

Their Champion Companion - the omnibus

DAWNBREAKER SERIES *SCI FI RH*

Voyage to Ayama

Dreaming of Ayama

THE LOST COVEN SERIES *PNR RH*

Aurora's Coven

Aurora's Betrayal

HER MONSTERS SERIES *PNR RH*

Rage

Hate

Book 3 *coming soon..*

THE FALLEN GODS SERIES *PNR*

Pretty Painful

Pretty Bloody

Pretty Stormy

Pretty Wild

Pretty Hot

Pretty Faces

Pretty Spelled

Fallen Gods - the omnibus 1

Fallen Gods - the omnibus 2

COURTS AND KINGS *PNR RH*

Court of Nightmares

Court of Death

Court of Beasts

Court of Heathens (Coming soon!)

FORBIDDEN READS *(STANDALONES)*

Daddy's Angel *CONTEMPORARY*

Stepbrothers' Darling *CONTEMPORARY RH*

LEGENDS AND LOVE *CONTEMPORARY*

Revolt

Rebel

PRETTY LIARS *CONTEMPORARY RH*

Unstoppable

Unbreakable

FORGOTTEN CITY *PNR*

Monstrous Lies

Monstrous Truths

Monstrous Ends

DEN OF VIPERS UNIVERSE STANDALONES

Scarlett Limerence *CONTEMPORARY*

Nadia's Salvation *CONTEMPORARY*

Alena's Revenge *CONTEMPORARY*

Den of Vipers *CONTEMPORARY RH*

Gangsters and Guns (Co-Write with Loxley Savage) *CONTEMPORARY RH*

STANDALONES

The Standby *CONTEMPORARY*

Diver's Heart *CONTEMPORARY RH*

Crown of Stars *SCI FI RH*

AUDIOBOOKS

The Wasteland

The Summit

Rage

Hate

Den of Vipers (*From Podium Audio*)

Gangsters and Guns (*From Podium Audio*)

Daddy's Angel (*From Podium Audio*)

Stepbrothers' Darling (*From Podium Audio*)

Blade of Iris (*From Podium Audio*)

Deadly Affair (*From Podium Audio*)

Deadly Match (*From Podium Audio*)

Deadly Encounter (*From Podium Audio*)

Stolen Trophy (*From Podium Audio*)

Crown of Stars (*From Podium Audio*)

Monstrous Lies (*From Podium Audio*)

Monstrous Truth (*From Podium Audio*)

Monstrous Ends (*From Podium Audio*)

Court of Nightmares (*From Podium Audio*)

Unstoppable (*From Podium Audio*)

Unbreakable (*From Podium Audio*)

Fractured Shadows (*From Podium Audio*)

SHARED WORLD PROJECTS

Blade of Iris - Mafia Wars *CONTEMPORARY RH*

CO-AUTHOR PROJECTS - *Erin O'Kane*

HER FREAKS SERIES *PNR Dystopian RH*

Circus Save Me

Taming The Ringmaster

Walking the Tightrope

Her Freaks Series - the omnibus

STANDALONES

The Hero Complex *PNR RH*

Dark Temptations *Collection of Short Stories, ft. One Night Only & Circus Saves Christmas*

THE WILD BOYS SERIES *CONTEMPORARY RH*

The Wild Interview

The Wild Tour

The Wild Finale

The Wild Boys - the omnibus

CO-AUTHOR PROJECTS - *Ivy Fox*

Deadly Love Series Contemporary

Deadly Affair

Deadly Match

Deadly Encounter

CO-AUTHOR PROJECTS - *Kendra Moreno*

STANDALONES

Stolen Trophy Contemporary RH

Fractured Shadows PNR RH

Burn Me PNR

CO-AUTHOR PROJECTS - *Loxley Savage*

THE FORSAKEN SERIES SCI FI RH

Capturing Carmen

Stealing Shiloh

Harboring Harlow

STANDALONES

Gangsters and Guns Contemporary, IN DEN OF VIPERS' UNIVERSE

OTHER CO-WRITES

Shipwreck Souls (*with Kendra Moreno & Poppy Woods*)

The Horror Emporium (*with Kendra Moreno & Poppy Woods*)

Find an error?

Please email this information to thenuttyformatter1@gmail.com:

- *the author name*
- *title of the book*
- *screenshot of the error*
- *suggested correction*